MW00807980

THE BEDMAKERS

CHAD LUTZKE
JOHN BODEN

Let the world know:
#IGotMyCLPBook!

Crystal Lake Publishing
www.CrystalLakePub.com

WELCOME
TO ANOTHER

CRYSTAL LAKE PUBLISHING
CREATION

Join today at www.crystallakepub.com & www.patreon.com/CLP

ACKNOWLEDGEMENTS

From Chad Lutzke:
Chad would like to thank: My wife Mary. Forever my muse, ideal reader, and greatest cheerleader. Abigail Suzanne Harszy and her grandfather Joseph Harszy Sr. for help with some grim details and a good laugh over a dark topic. Joe Mynhardt for taking a chance on our book. John Boden . . . what beautiful music we make together. Always seamless, always easy. I'm so proud of what we've done here, always am. My awesome patrons: Mike Perez, Shannon Bradner, Glenda Magner, Mathieu Fortin, George "Book Monster" Ranson, Liane Abe, Steve Gracin, Night Worms (Sadie Hartmann and Ashley Saywers), Shannan Ross, Wayne Fenlon, Jamie Goecker, Melissa Potter, Christian Berntsen, Jerri Nall, Danielle Milton, Mary Kiefel, Alyssa Manning, Dirk Gard, Lee-ann Oleski, Steve Pattee, Janelle Janson, Holly Rae Garcia, Phillip Frangules, Crystal Lake Publishing (Joe Mynhardt), Crystal Staley, Hunter Shea, Kristyn Kasper, Sheila Porter, Cynthia Moon, Jon Cowles, Justas Grigas, Steve Barnard, Missy Kritzer, Tina True Edwards, Alexis Vieira, Kristina Osborne, Renee Barry, Audra Stinson, and Nicole Rubbo.

From John Boden:
Chad Lutzke, one of my favorite partners in crime. We work in entirely different ways but our eyes share the same vision and our hearts the same beats sometimes. I love you, brother!

My Mom and brother, including my adopted brother, Mike. My wife and sons, Elton Nestler-one of my oldest friends, Bob Ford, Ken Wood—I'd not be writing a damn thing if you hadn't kick started me when I was stalled. Sadie Hartmann, so many people . . . if I know you, I thank you. If I don't I thank you too.

CHAPTER 1

Chicago, 1979

THE OLD MAN bent and tied his shoe, double knots to ensure his shuffling gait wouldn't free the hard work. The wooden bench beneath him moaned from the shift in weight. His knuckles puffed with arthritis like the long necks of geese plugged with apples. Such simple tasks brought on a deep mourning for youth, and he wondered if that particular chore was harder for him or for the uncoordinated, chubby digits of a three-year-old.

He unsheathed a knife and cracked his face with a lopsided grin at the sheen of the blade—a sense of pride in his upkeep of the WWII relic. Saw his reflection in it, and the smile faded like the youth he possessed when first obtaining the weapon. He looked up at the sallow sky and nodded at its uncaring countenance, something he was used to.

Before the bus came, the knife was back in its home, and the old man counted the change in his pocket for the third time. He wouldn't need a transfer. They were free for senior citizens, but exact change was important. He would have no one waiting behind him while he counted the coins with the speed of chilled honey. His pride didn't allow for such things any more than the thin patience of others.

The man unbuttoned the plaid, wool coat that would be too hot by noon and stared at his feet as he considered rolling up the legs of his old Dickies. Too much work. He'd be on the hunt for clothes, maybe even spring for something at a yard sale. But for now, he'd keep his pants bunched at the waist under frayed rope and the legs trapped under his heels. Just so long as they didn't interfere with the damn laces.

The bank clock across the street read seven twenty. He was to meet Calvin at eight on 32nd and Lincoln. Lord willing, day-old

It was a short walk to 32nd and Lincoln. So short, in fact, that if his eyes were twenty years younger, he just might make out Calvin Gunning up ahead, ass on an empty wooden crate, back propped against Joe & Dough's sandy-brick wall.

Genie went through a mental checklist of reassurance. Looked at his laces. Still intact. Cinched the rope-belt. Tight, snug. Patted his coat for the knife. All was well.

He showed the world a smile, his face toward the blue-orange sky. The smile was fake and plastic these days, but any smile was a kind of thankful prayer. And he imagined God shining down on him with approval. It was all the reward he needed.

When Genie arrived, Calvin was busy stacking a set of four dice the color of cloudy urine, doing his best to balance a donut hole on top of them. He'd already hit the dumpster and had Genie's breakfast laid out on a strip of restroom paper towel.

Like Genie, Calvin wore a pair of old Dickies. But his fit like God himself had seamed them. A worn army jacket with a hole on the sleeve where a patch once sat covered him, and the top of his head shone in the morning sun where hair had betrayed him years ago. The rest of his dome was covered in wiry, gray tufts that he'd rub often, the prickle of it itching calloused palms.

"Slowpoke," Calvin said, his dark eyes still on the balancing act. "I ate the custard."

"You know that's a bad idea."

"Couldn't help it. She's a seductress."

"She ain't worth it. I give you two hours before you're on the pot, knees to chin, cursing her."

"Maybe." He handed Genie a lidless cup of coffee that was still warm.

"From Wilson?"

Calvin nodded. "Fresh brew. He's in an unusually good mood today."

"Musta gotten some tail."

"Musta."

Genie took the cup and sipped at it. Wiry hairs from his upper lip dipped into the brown liquid and collected drops, which were quickly swept away by a thirsty tongue. He dipped the not-too-stale pastry into his cup, then pushed it into his mouth. It helped if the things he ate were softer. His pearly whites weren't much of either pastries would be waiting undisturbed atop the dumpster at Wilson's Joe & Dough—an unspoken deal they had with the owner. Then it was off to the parking lot behind the theater. Four acres of pavement that brought drunken college students on the weekends, leaving their empties behind. A small fortune camouflaged as refuse.

Mondays were good to him.

The bus rolled up, then squeaked to a halt, as though whatever pushed the rusting thing screamed under the pressure of each stop. He pulled the exact change from his pocket, climbed the bus steps, and deposited the coins, then shuffled down the ribbed aisle. He sat near the back in an empty seat that exhaled the sour breath from the asses of Chicago through tears in the vinyl.

Two seats up on his left sat Margaret. She saw him, and he nodded. Her smile was probably something brighter once, but now it was black caves among splintered bone, her dark, beady eyes set deep in the old catcher's mitt that was the rest of her face. She could have passed for a century old. The sun's licking, and the drink, made sure of that.

She smoothed greasy hair with a palsied hand and smiled at him. "Eugene MacDowell, as I live an' breathe." Her words were edge-worn things in an old drawer.

The aging man rose, ran fingers through thinning, tightly curled hair that was somehow still darker than the gray that overtook his beard, and moved up to take the seat beside hers. "Hi, Margie." He patted her swollen knee with a gnarled hand. "How you been, Doll?"

"Keep suckin' air. Some days I find that a comfort, others a curse." She smiled bigger, but it was not matched by her almond eyes. They were things that swam the sea. They knew salt water.

Genie nodded. "I know how that is." He looked down at her pale and dirty legs and the veins that bulged there, thick and blue like map lines. He noted the tip of a scratch just above the edge of her sock, saw the angry red of it. Saw the blackening kiss around the edge of the tight skin. Noticed the darkened stain of the cotton that tried to hide it. He sadly pursed his lips and patted her knee once more. "I'm off at the next stop. Margie, you take care now. I'll see you around." He stood and shuffled up the aisle to stand and wait for the bus to slow, then stop. He looked back at the old woman and waved, knowing he'd probably never lay eyes on her again, but smiled anyway and got off the bus.

these days. Cadaver gray and soft as aspirin. He did his best to keep after them, though, stole a toothbrush from a bin a while back, and after an overnight soak in bleach, he rinsed it in water and had himself a bona fide article of personal upkeep.

"What's the plan?" Calvin popped the donut hole he'd been playing with into his mouth and chewed loudly.

"You know I prefer to work without a net." Genie winked and swallowed the last of the tepid coffee. He tossed the cup into the open dumpster and took out an old pen he kept in his shirt pocket. After touching the tip to a pale tongue, he wrote a note of heartfelt thanks on the paper towel and slid it under the back door of Wilson's Joe and Dough. He stood and leaned back far enough to crack his spine, minuscule gunshots from between old bones. "I did hear tell there's honest work out west."

"I'm not goin' to California. I ain't truckin' with hippies." Calvin was dead serious in his indignation.

"Hell, not that far. From where we're sittin', damn near everything's west. I was thinkin' maybe farmland west. Maybe a little further."

Calvin nodded and fished a cigarette from his vest. He rolled his own, and while this may have been a thing of precise beauty when he made it, it was bent as a witch's finger. He stuck it between cold-cracked lips and lit it with an old lighter he'd found on the ground outside a store. His eye had been drawn to the large-mouth bass on the side of it, splashing free from the water. It reminded him of pleasant times. As the blueish smoke fled his nostrils, he spoke. "Can't be worse than here, I guess."

"Don't believe in guesses. You know that. A guess is a wish that didn't try hard enough."

"So I've heard." Calvin breathed the smoke he told himself too many times he'd part from. "I'm quitting smoking. This here's my last one." He nodded to Genie and then looked pensively at the ground. "We talkin' trains?"

"We're talkin' whatever it takes."

"'Cept hippies."

"I'm not ruling it out, but I hear your grievances. And I'd be lying if I didn't share them. But I'll be damned if a kid with a flower in his mop is gonna stop me from livin'. And if breathin' reefer for an afternoon gets me to better days, well then, I suppose I've done worse for less. 'Sides, these days I think the kids done curled the

4

locks up tight to their head like mine. Even white folk got 'fros these days, tradin' flowers for dancin' shoes."

Calvin nodded, tossed his cup in the dumpster, ground the end of the smoke on the cement, and dropped it in as well.

"So it's settled," Genie said it with a smack to the pavement, a declaration that sealed the deal.

"Grab our things?"

Genie answered with the popping of his knees as he stood.

"I might smoke my last cigarette on the way," Calvin muttered, and Genie rolled his eyes, shook his head.

CHAPTER 2

GENIE RELEASED ANOTHER sigh into the air. He imagined an entire layer of them ringing the planet like clouds of desperation and disdain. He closed the flap of the old, canvas suitcase and zipped it, all his earthly possessions safe inside. After stowing it by the stack of dry-rotted tires near the mouth of the alley, he dragged two wooden pallets over by the trio of dented trash cans behind the hardware store. They had served as wall and roof for the last few weeks, and he was grateful for them and the dry weather. He leaned the pallets against the wall and hoped they'd come in handy for another needy soul. There was no shortage of them in the world, and if his intuition was anything to be believed, there never would be.

Almost as an afterthought, he took a pen from his pocket and wrote *Genie was here '79* on the faded wood of the nearest pallet, followed by a smiley face sporting an unruly beard. He grinned as he walked back over to the suitcase, smoothed down the strips of black tape that sealed the wound in its side, and picked it up. His entire life weighed less than ten pounds.

While Calvin gathered his own things, Genie left for Washington Bridge, just two blocks away. Calvin knew why. His friend was saying goodbye to Louise. She and Genie had been an item, even without a home. The romance had died years ago, but they remained close, even closer than when they were holding one another, wrapped in the glow of trash-barrel fires.

When Genie met Louise, she'd been down on her luck for nearly as long as they had, but you'd never guess it. A brush and makeup were among her most valuable possessions. Not once would she start a day without beautifying herself. And before the day withered, she'd touch up whatever necessary. Unlike most near the bridge, she had still cared. Most near the bridge were filled with pessimism, husks packed with compost that bitched and moaned like it was the only words they knew. But Louise, she was missing that bone.

After Calvin packed his bag, he sat on a cinderblock with his back against the fence, having prayer-like thoughts directed toward his knees, hoping they were ready for the trek ahead and the work demanded of them once they found it. If they found it.

Genie showed up with his head down, cradling his suitcase and rubbing a thumb over the tape. Calvin walked over, shrinking the space between them, then grabbed Genie's shoulder and squeezed. "Said your goodbyes?"

"For real this time, I'm thinkin'."

Calvin said nothing, just rose to stand with his friend as they worked up the nerve to take the first steps toward an uncertain future.

CHAPTER 3

THEY HEADED FOR the tracks. A train was always the plan should they ever find the gumption to leave. It was free—relying heavily on an open and vacant boxcar going the right way—and less wear on their feet. The boots they both wore were meant to last, but the miles on them had already exceeded expectations, and should they fall apart, there'd be no complaint. They'd been loyal. Much like their hearts, as well as their bones.

The old leather on their feet had been issued within the same year, courtesy of the U.S. Army. Calvin had worn his longer, prouder, while Genie kept his in the closet in trade for loafers, when life was normal. Before PTSD crept in. Before Janice left. Before pieces stopped fitting as snugly as they ought to. A scenario that was a hobbling doppelganger to Calvin's own.

It was a four-block walk to the tracks. These particular tracks were the safest to jump, as the train made a quick stop six days a week. There were other tracks, but Derrick Matthews had lost both legs attempting a hop there, showing off after a bottle of Mad Dog. He was humbled right quick, though played it tough, barking things like, "Legs ain't good for nothin' but runnin' anyway!" between swigs of tepid rue from discarded bottles.

The train's schedule wasn't like clockwork, but you could count on early morning, and then again around noon. Give or take an hour. And time was something they never ran short of.

Trains also passed through the wee hours, when the sun still had the blanket pulled over its face. But the men had agreed on the predictability of a daylight ride. Besides, it was a night train that took Derrick Matthews' legs. Maybe even his manhood, though he never mentioned it. It's not something you wheel around bragging about.

The two men arrived and sat on the ground near the tracks.

Calvin grabbed a handful of rocks and made aim for the crossing sign, tossing one at a time. "You feeling regret?" he asked, between the gong-like *bongs* of the rocks striking metal.

"Regret? My feet ain't even left the ground yet."

"I saw the way you were back there." His smile tripped and faltered slightly. "Lookin' like you might miss home."

"Not sure I'd call that home, but don't you worry none about me. These old wings are ready to fly. The cobwebs and dust can blow right off." He chuckled, but Calvin didn't echo it.

"Can blow off just as easy when you're falling as it can when you're flyin' high and free."

Bong!

Genie tried for a smile, but it melted into something too weak to stand on its own. For far too long, life had felt like just that—falling. "You're never too old," he mumbled out loud, but the words were meant for him only. A new mantra.

"What's that?"

"We're not washed up. Not just yet." Genie halfway scowled and fiddled with the end of his scarf. The scarf wasn't as firm as it used to be, more of a comforting old thing that fit close and snug like a familiar shirt.

"Hell, if I believed we were anywhere near, I wouldn't be sittin' here with you ready to cross the country like some damn hippie."

Bong!

As they waited, neither of them spoke of fear, even though it hovered over like a murder of crows.

※※※

The noonish train came much later than usual, and by the time the tracks rumbled and the approaching engine howled, both men were hungry again. Hopping the train now meant skipping a meal, maybe two. But grumbling bellies or not, the time to move was now.

Genie hopped up from the spot they'd sat for hours, his ass damp from the grass. He brushed the clumps of dirt and twigs from it as he jogged to the rise where the track was. He looked back and watched Calvin take the small hill in three steps. Calvin was shorter, his legs eating less distance, though neither man was spry as they'd been even a decade ago.

They stood and watched as the engine rounded the bend, then

leaned back in case the engineer was watching and happened to give a shit. The train rolled by, slowing for the switch, and it struck Calvin how much like a monster it looked—an enormous steel worm with one giant nostril that threatened a shot of dragon's fire. He turned and saw Genie was side-stepping down the line a ways. The cars slowed and the brakes hissed and the engine stopped by the switch. Genie and Calvin held their breath and watched the engineer hop down and make his way to the lever beside the red-light pole.

"Now," Genie whispered, and tossed his suitcase into an open car. He jumped in, then turned to extend a hand. Calvin offered the duffel, and Genie tossed it behind, then gave his hand again and helped his friend inside.

They rolled back in the shadows and lay still, heard the crunch of gravel underfoot and the ragged hawking of the driver's throat, followed by a wad of spit hitting stone. A tattered voice singing about blue eyes crying in the rain rose outside the car and then faded along with the footsteps. All was silent and stalled for long minutes before the gears groaned and the wheels began to roll. Before they knew it, the landscape whirled by like a faded painting on a spool being unwound at high speed.

"Just like life," Calvin muttered.

Genie clapped a hand on his friend's back and nodded. "Here and then gone."

CHAPTER 4

IT WASN'T LONG before the men were sharing a sheet of cardboard folded under them. Twenty years earlier, hell, ten, and they could hold up just fine against the bounce of the tracks, but these days muscle grew lean and gave way to bone, making the bumpy ride damn painful.

"This ass-on-wood bullshit . . . " Genie shifted impatiently, trying to get comfortable.

"Hmm mmm," Calvin grumbled like it was a tired amen.

Genie watched the blur of trees as they passed through a wooded area and smiled. "Despite the ass beatin', makes ya feel young again. Up and leaving, no true destination. Amblin'."

"Sounds like hippie talk."

"Shit, don't you start."

"Maybe at the next stop, we can grab you a flower right quick. You can put it in your hair. We can buy you some reefer and beads and some of them bellbottoms." Calvin chuckled through the words.

Genie threw into the mix his own wet laughter. His lungs coated everything with an oily sound these days.

But Genie was right. There was something about the journey, about facing the unknown, that lifted the spirit and made him feel young again. Even in his bones, he could feel it. And they'd need all the youthful vigor they could get. They knew when heading out that any work available would be laborious, nothing sedentary. And it'd either kill them or return some long-lost health, which seemed to have blown away like so much ash—atrophied muscle, rusty joints. Health or death, they were ready for either. And if health didn't come, may as well be the end. Do them a favor. That's how Calvin saw it. Bring it or end it. But dammit, make something happen. Shuffling around idly, looking for food, ain't no way for a man to live.

··*

Nearly eight hours into the journey, the scent of pine triggered a brief smile across Genie's face. It'd been a while. Only other scent that helped him escape these past several years was the perfume Louise wore. He wasn't sure what it was called, but it had the power to brighten the darkest day, if even for just a moment.

He rubbed the orange scarf around his neck. It'd been a gift from her. He recalled the day she gave it. Louise was sitting on an old kitchen chair near a patch of weeds, its metal legs dappled with rust and the vinyl covering torn in places. The patch was like a wild garden in the middle of a concrete desert. Paper tumbleweeds and Styrofoam stones. Napkins and newsprint splayed against cement like dead birds. She was knitting the scarf, using yarn donated by the fabric store on 32nd. She'd sell the scarves, mittens, and some potholders, for next to nothing and more often than not just give them away.

"Morning, Louise."

She'd looked up, squinted against the sun, her smile being the best part of that day. "It is, isn't it?" The smile stuck there, glowing.

"I like that color." Genie pointed at the orange scarf in her lap.

"That's good, 'cause it's yours." She beamed.

"Oh, I couldn't . . . "

"Don't start with the humble shit, Genie. You'll take it and you'll wear it. You'll be thanking me come December."

Now, Genie fought back tears—flaring nostrils and gritting teeth. A promised meal and comfortable bed was something he lacked, but the gratitude he held for the simple things was boundless. Having nothing to call your own does that to you.

He opened his suitcase and fetched a stack of paper and a pen. The paper was nothing more than a brown paper bag cut into sheets, then pressed flat by one of many cinder blocks near the bridge, or by his own ass. The pen (three of them, actually) came by way of a visit to the bank. While Genie wasn't in the habit of stealing, taking from a bank didn't really count. After all, thieving was what banks did best, and thieving from the thieves ain't much thieving at all.

He held down the top left corner of the sheet with a calloused thumb and forefinger and stared at the void of it. A blank space waiting for words. He closed his eyes and watched them swimming around in the bowl of his brain, like little fish he couldn't grasp with feeble fingers. He breathed deeply through his nose, calmed himself. The words swam slower, and he could see them clearly. His eyes seemed to stare through the back of his hand, brown skin dotted with a constellation of pink scars and freshly introduced age spots. He blinked rapidly a few times to refocus and felt a smile drift to his lips as he touched the stolen pen to thick paper and wrote the dawn of a letter by the light of the moon.

"*Dear Louise . . .*"

The script lilted like the warped mast of a derelict ship. He smelled salt and despair as the words flowed from him, a font that would not be quelled. His teeth ached from the set of his jaw, and the words bounded from brain to hand, through pen to pressed wood pulp, in a dangerous dance. The corner of the boxcar was quiet, save for the rodential scritch of ink on paper, the furtive breaths that puffed from his mouth, and the rustle and clank from the wheels on the rails. Under the blanket of all this, Calvin slept.

Genie packed his hobo stationary back into his bag, along with the pen, then pulled a folded piece of paper from his shirt pocket, something he'd read more times than he cared to remember. In fact, he didn't even need to unfold it, not really.

He read the doctor's note, going over the diagnosis. It made little sense to be handed such a card after the deck he'd been given the past decade or more. But in hindsight, he supposed there was some rationale. You don't smoke for forty years and walk away unscathed. Might've been that, coupled with smoke from the war, solar rays from the sun, who knew? But a terminal disease? It didn't seem fair, considering.

He closed the paper, so worn and lined it nearly folded itself now, then returned it to his shirt pocket. Right next to his traitorous lungs. Ironically appropriate. He buttoned the pocket, keeping the only secret he had from his good friend hidden behind a thin layer of flannel.

CHAPTER 5

"**M**ORNIN' SWEETHEART," Calvin crowed as he stirred whatever was cooling in the old coffee can. He had managed to make a small fire in the boxcar using an old tin pan and debris clotted in the corners, resting the can in the center. The fire lived only a few short minutes.

Genie sniffed hard and cocked an eyebrow. "What is that?"

"Soup. Sorta." Calvin stirred it with a twig, pulling it out and touching the tip to his tongue. "Ain't too good either . . . but I suspect it'll stave off the rumbles."

"What's in it exactly?" Genie scooted closer on his knees and peered into the slow-boiling depths of the can, like a witch.

"A couple of taters I found in the corner. I cut out the squishy bits. Found an onion too, and maybe a piece of carrot . . . or an old pencil eraser. Regardless, I added some shakes from our salt and pepper."

Genie looked at the old tin, saw it filled with ash. "And you tried cooking it."

"For a few. Wasn't much to burn, but I managed to get the food a step closer to lukewarm."

"Not as pretty as them cookin' ladies on the TV, but you'll do."

Genie slapped the smaller man's back, and they laughed together. After their breakfast soup, which was every bit as tragic and gross as both had suspected, the men sat and reminisced. They took turns positing what the future and their adventures might yield and fell into odd valleys of silence. During those moments, Genie struggled with keeping silent about the spreading rot in his lungs but thought of the burden it might cause. He didn't want that. He wanted things to be how they once were. Not necessarily the days where a bed was guaranteed but when freedom was. No black clouds lingered. No aching bones and strange pains. There was still some youth buried under that leathered flesh.

While Calvin watched the blur of trees with heavy lids, Genie wrote yet another note to Louise and, with his knife, whittled one of the twigs down to nothing more than a toothpick.

The train rolled on, and time with it.

※※※

The train rolled to a stop. Trees stood sporadically, dotting the open plains in front of them. Genie peeked his head out of the train-car and saw more trees one way and what looked like a factory the other.

"Any mountains?" Calvin asked.

"If there is, they're hidden. How long you figure we been riding?"

"My bones say a lifetime, but the sun says a good eighteen hours, at least."

"Damn." Genie rubbed his backside and surveyed the terrain. "The land's flatter than an old tit, smack dab in tornado valley."

"Alley . . . tornado alley," Calvin mumbled. All the bouncing had been hard on his bones, and he was saltier than an Easter ham. "I wouldn't mind jumpin' here."

"And get swept away by a twister? You're off your nut! Hell, folks get thrown around by them sonsofbitches even with a roof over their head, never mind without."

Calvin gripped the door and pulled himself up. "Genie, it's clear as crystal. Not a cloud in the sky."

"Hell no. 'Sides, further west is where the work's at."

"You seem awfully sure on that."

"People migrate there. The more people, the more jobs." Genie sounded like he was reading from a cue card.

"The more jobs already taken."

Genie seemed to consider the logic, then brushed it off. It was a dream killer that had no business here. "Okay . . . let's stretch the legs a bit, give the ass a rest."

Calvin was climbing out before Genie even capped the statement with a period. Genie followed.

With belongings in hand, the two walked alongside the train and peeked in between the cars, wishing for mountains they knew wouldn't be there. Instead, they saw two children playing at the tree line, sticks in their hands, as though they were swords, and battling one another, being careful not to cause any real damage.

The two men watched them. "Youth don't last forever," Calvin said.

"Sometimes it barely begins." Genie turned and walked along the train and toward a road up ahead. Calvin followed.

The sound of kicked gravel played as a soundtrack against the quiet as the two made their way toward nothing in particular. Once past the caboose, they spotted a strip of buildings across the street in the distance, one of which was clearly a diner.

"We got enough money to get some eats? Like *real* eats?" Calvin asked.

Genie pulled out the thin thing that was his wallet, opened it. He removed a five-dollar bill and held it out to Calvin. "If we can feed both of us for this, we do."

Calvin's eyes lit up. "You been holding out?"

"Found it on the bus last week. Remember that asshole I was tellin' you about? The one what carved the swastika in the seat? Karma pulled it from his pocket, threw it right on the ground. I didn't have the heart to tell him." Genie's face cracked with a grin.

"Coulda scored some points with the Reich."

"Fuck 'em."

They walked to the edge of the train yard and started on a sidewalk that materialized out of weeds and gravel. The sun was warm and the sky still clear. And while they were starving and tired and their bones were achy, their thoughts were on those kids and the many years they still had ahead.

CHAPTER 6

THE GRAVY WAS RICH. Calvin savored it as long as possible before swallowing. The fiver had gotten them each an open-faced roast beef sandwich smothered in gravy and a bowl of mashed potatoes. Genie had done the math and surmised the waitress had been a kind one who knew hungry when she bellied up to it. He stared at his empty plate, still hungry but grateful.

Calvin watched a little boy play with a noodle from his plate of spaghetti. His mouth raised in a half-smile when the kid finally got it to his mouth and slurped with great flair. Even the smile couldn't betray the weariness in his features. "So . . . where do we go from here?"

"I don't even know where here is," Genie responded. He looked at the menu, then smiled. "The Farm Stove Diner."

"Cutely quaint. But no, I mean back on the train and further west. Or should we throw our dice here and see how they roll?"

Genie pondered this as he worried at the string of beef caught between his back teeth. He side-eyed the front window and saw the clear sky start to dim. His strong desire to break from the train trumped his fear of tornadoes. "What say we spend tonight in a park? It's clear and warm yet. And we can talk until we fall asleep, start fresh tomorrow."

"Damned if you couldn't sell lighter fluid to the Devil, Genie. We're gonna do the same shit we was doing back east, yet you make it sound like a reward."

"It is. Livin' to see another day."

The men rose, and Genie stood at the register counter, waited for the young lady to give him her attention. Calvin nodded at her and mouthed the words *thank you* and exited to wait out front.

Genie held out the wrinkled five-dollar bill, and the girl took it. She held it lower than the register and hit a button or two, then another to make the drawer open. She handed the five back to Genie and smiled at him. "Your change, Sir. Thank you, and please come again." She pushed the bill into his hand and made a point to touch his fingers. "God bless."

"Indeed, sometimes. Thank you, Ma'am."

He turned and walked out of The Farm Stove Diner, blessing in hand.

CHAPTER 7

CALVIN HELD A hand above his brow, scanning the flat land. "So, you mentioned a park. We supposed to sniff one out, or you see something I didn't?"

"It may have been wishful thinking."

Calvin grumbled.

Genie spotted a small cloud in the distance—a nonthreatening slice of cotton. "But now that I think on it, I'd rather not stick around, park or otherwise."

"Yer still afraid of a twister, aren't ya?" The bright blue above seemed to laugh right along with Calvin.

"They can sneak up on ya. The sky ain't always something to be trusted."

"Well, you may have to put a little faith in her, cuz I don't think we're catching our ride." Calvin pointed toward the trainyard, where a length of steel was pulling out and heading west.

"Ahh, hell."

The two kicked dust with ancient boots, making their way toward the train at least a hundred yards away.

"We'll never make it!" Calvin yelled.

"Quit gabbin' and save your breath." Genie's voice was a fistful of leaves.

The train blasted its outgoing shout, smoke billowed, and the beast picked up speed. The two men's jangly run lasted all of twenty seconds before giving up.

With hands on knees and burning lungs, Genie cursed at their luck. "I swear . . . if it all ends with us mixin' flesh with a cow in the sky on account of God's wrath . . . "

Calvin dropped to his ass, catching his own breath. "Enough with the twister shit, old man. We've faced worse."

"Our whole life's been a storm, huh?"

"Along with a helluva drought here and there. But this is good for us, Genie. This runnin' . . . this fear. The work ahead will kick our ass, no doubt. But ain't nobody lived a good, long life sittin' on their ass. It'll be like taking a drink from the fountain of youth."

Genie hacked a thick piece of dark phlegm, shot it across the road and into the grass. "Yeah," was all he said.

The two hunted for a place to sleep near the yard, keeping their eyes on incoming trains, with the intention of hopping the first to come along, just so long as it was heading west.

Genie insisted on sleeping in a gulley. Calvin knew it had everything to do with tornado paranoia. Gullies were the safest bet if shelter wasn't near. So he humored his friend and made camp just off the road within a thin line of trees and meadow grass.

They made an unnecessary fire using dead grass and twigs, then spent the rest of daylight with more reminiscing and dreams about the future.

Once again, Genie nearly told his friend about the burden he carried in his pocket, but that albatross was his own, and not the kind of thing you present when struggling for a spark to start anew. News like that would be a thorn in Calvin's side, just as much as his own.

Finally, shadows crept like ebony fingers across the gulley, as the sun said goodnight and swapped shifts with the moon. The trainyard had remained still throughout the day, save for a handful of men smoking cigarettes and trading laughs during breaks outside a loading dock. Genie and Calvin pretended they weren't growing hungry again. Something they were good at.

The two sat shoulder-to-shoulder against a tree, and just like Genie had promised, they talked until sleep came.

CHAPTER 8

GENIE WOKE WITH a hand in his pants pocket. Not his hand. Not Calvin's either, but that of someone he couldn't quite see. He sat still, his eyes open wide, straining to catch any detail from the shape in front of him. When the moonlight caught a pair of glasses, he acted. With agility that surprised even himself, Genie went for the pen in his shirt, pulled it out, then swung down into the black mass. The pen sunk inches deep, triggering a scream. The mass jumped back and into the moonlight. There stood a slim man with specs and a thin, bearded face, gripping his arm.

"You . . . you stabbed me!" he said.

"I got another, you wanna try me."

Calvin shot up, balled his fists in front of him. "What's goin' on? You all right, Genie?"

"This shithead was tryin' to rob us. Or he was searching for my willy."

"Aww, damn, this stings." The pen still jutted from the man's upper arm. A thin stream of glistening black crept down his shirt.

"We look like we got anything worth stealin', jackass?" Calvin asked. His breathing was loud and his nostrils flaring, both signs that the fuse was burning short.

"Was worth a shot . . . dammit." The man breathed pain through his teeth.

At the sound of an approaching train, both Genie and Calvin stood up, gathered their things.

"Gonna need that pen back," Genie said. And before the man could argue, Genie's hand was on it, pulling the pen from the hole it'd made.

"Sonofabitch!" the man yelled.

"Next time the mood strikes ya, keep your hands to yourself. You're lucky I used the pen and not my knife."

Calvin tossed in a "Jackass," and the two jogged toward the trainyard, while the bearded man whimpered behind them.

This time, the train never stopped, only slowed to a crawl for all of sixty seconds before taking off again, just enough time for them to hop in an open car and lay back, crashing from the adrenaline rush.

As they stared at the black abyss of the car's ceiling, catching their breath, Calvin spoke first. "Would you have done it?"

"Killed him?" Genie said through a raspy wheeze. "If it meant us or him."

"Hell, I don't know that I've got it in me anymore, Genie. If it came down to it."

"Don't any of us know until the moment. I remember the first time I faced that dilemma. The will to live takes over. Ain't no time to think."

"Big difference when you're stuck in a war and being told to kill."

"Yeah, I suppose you're right."

A quick blink of lightning lit a cloud in the distance. "Told ya," Genie said when he saw it.

"Lightning doesn't mean a twister's comin'."

"Don't mean it's not, either."

A rustling fluttered from far in the dark corner of the car, and the two men went silent, turning their attention to the sound, each of them squinting through the black. This had happened before, jumping a occupied car and finding out too late they were sharing a ride with a drunk covered in his own urine.

"Hello?" Genie said.

Whispers from the corner like mice scurrying. A face came into the dim curtain of moonlight.

Then another.

CHAPTER 9

WITH THE FIRST FACE, Genie expected to see rugged scruff with drunken, jaundiced eyes peeking out from the darkness. But what came forth was the smooth, baby face of a teenage boy. "Hey," the boy whispered. His eyes were saucer-wide, and the skin under them held a deep purple, like he hadn't slept all week. He wore a hat that looked like it belonged on a forest ranger, with a patch of the American flag sewed on the side, upside down.

The two old men traded glances, then spoke back in unison. "Hey . . . "

The other face was thinner, almost gaunt. This boy wore a baseball cap turned backward with duct tape holding it together and what looked like the beginnings of a goatee hanging from his pointy chin. "Where you fellas headed?" he said.

"Uhh . . . west." Genie felt both sad and excited for the boys. Being young on such an adventure seemed like time well spent, learning about life in a way no one person could teach you. But what of their parents? Were these runaways, with worried-sick parents sitting by the phone?

"You cool?" the forest ranger asked.

"Are we cool?" Calvin looked at Genie. "Yeah, we're cool."

"Right on," Forest Ranger said, then moved out of the shadows completely and squatted down next to Calvin, while the other boy crawled over near the open door and sat looking out.

Both boys looked nervous, and Genie figured he would too at that age, seeing how two strange men just hopped their train, at night, with no way off but tumbling out at fifty mph.

"So . . . where are you boys headed?" Genie asked.

"Just on for a quick ride."

"What's yer name, kid?" Calvin said. He was talking to the gaunt boy staring out the door.

"His name's Simon," Forest Ranger said.

"He a mute?"

"Nah. He's just seasick. He gets like that sometimes."

"We call it The Tilt," Genie said. "Train tilting this way, your brain tilting the other. You get used to it. Like being on a ship."

"And you? What's yer name?" Calvin asked.

"Uhh . . . Tony."

Something about the way he said it made Genie think the kid was lying. Again, he didn't blame him. For all the boys knew, he and Calvin were gonna beat them senseless and take their clothes.

"I'm Eugene."

"Calvin." The old man nodded and patted his chest.

"Soo . . . what's out west?" Tony said.

"A new start. Hopefully."

The gaunt boy turned his hat around, pulled it down so the bill hid his eyes.

"You guys gonna be gettin' off at the next stop or ridin' through?" Tony pulled a cigarette from a pack that looked like it'd been stepped on. Popped it between his thin lips and slid his hand into his pocket, coming out with a pack of matches like some magic trick.

"Never can tell," Calvin said, his eyes never leaving that fresh cigarette in the boy's mouth. "The weather, an empty belly, giving the ole ass a break. They're all factors."

Simon stared out of the car at nothing in particular. In the moon's glow, his cheeks looked wet beneath the eyes.

"You sure your buddy's okay?" Genie asked.

"He'll be fine. Don't worry about him." Tony sucked smoke from the crooked cigarette and blew it from his nostrils like a dragon.

Lightning flashed, closer this time, and thunder came with it. Looked like they were riding straight into the eye of a storm. The spatter of rain speckled Calvin's boots, and he brought his feet up near his ass.

"You boys ever seen a twister?" Genie stuck his hand out to feel the rain and how much the wind had picked up.

"You scared?" Tony lit a match and tried lighting a second cigarette, but the growing wind denied it.

"Nah," Genie lied.

"Seems like you are. If we do hit one, best bet is to lie in a ditch. This train's a deathtrap."

Genie swallowed hard and felt his asshole loosen, his sphincter going on strike, while the wind howled a banshee's cry.

"Ain't no twister comin' through!" Calvin had to shout over the storm's boisterous moan. "It's just like any other storm! Thunder, lightning, wind! We been through a million of 'em!"

Genie appreciated Calvin's effort, but he wasn't convinced. Not with how fast the wind had picked up. He wondered if the sky was green under all that black, and he waited for the lightning to strike again, seeing if he could catch a glimpse of the sky's true color.

Simon staring off like that reminded Genie of when a person hears news they can't handle, and they just shut down. Something decidedly off about it.

"You sure you're okay!?" Genie asked him. Simon was a statue.

Lightning cracked, and the car lit up with a quick flash. Out of his peripheral, Genie caught sight of another figure, tucked back in the corner where the boys had come from. Something lying down.

Or crawling.

Lightning hit again, but this time Genie was watching the corner. Everything he wasn't sure he saw came into view. And there was no denying what it was.

"Cal!" he yelled.

Silent Simon swung around and faced Genie. "He's right! It's a deathtrap! And there *is* a tornado coming! You should get in a ditch, or you're gonna die!" His eyes were like two eggs marked with a single hole in the center.

"What?!" Calvin called out, but the wind snatched the word, swallowing it whole.

Genie wasn't sure what scared him more, the prospect of an incoming twister, the thing in the corner, or the boy's eyes, with that unexpected spray of strange words filled with an almost demonic excitement.

After catching the intensity on the boy's face, Calvin balled his fist out of instinct. "What's goin' on, Genie?"

The boy swung his head back to the open door, and the wind rushed in like God himself was trying to tip the train over, violently stirring every hair on every head in a wave of chaos.

"There's a girl over there!" Genie pointed toward the corner. "She's—"

"Get in the fucking ditch!" Simon grabbed Genie's leg with both hands and pulled him toward the open door.

It took Genie a second before he realized the kid was actually trying to throw him off the train. This teenaged, wide-eyed bastard.

Best case scenario, Genie'd break some bones, probably several. And if he was lucky enough, he'd be found before starving to death or rotting from the inside out with internal bleeding, right there next to the tracks.

His big hands planted themselves on the floor, and he yanked his foot back. But Simon came with it, and that's when Tony joined in. The kid grabbed Genie's other leg and pulled as hard as he could, digging his fingers into the tendons behind Genie's knee.

Before Calvin could get to either of the boys, Genie's head hit the floor of the car, and he slid at least two feet toward the door. The large knife he carried fell from his pocket and slid across the floor toward the door, where any moment the wind would suck the weapon out.

The wind screamed, the lightning crashed, and the train swayed. This had to have been a twister, but that fear was long gone. The real threat was two kids who meant to kill him. Kids he could have put a fierce whooping on, even at his age, had they not jumped him.

The one boy was trying his damnedest to pull Genie's hamstring from his leg, like they were old guitar strings that needed replacing. The man groaned through his teeth, grabbing at the smooth floor for anything to help stop him from flying out the door, his nails digging in the wood, splinters pushing deep. And no matter how hard he tried pulling back his legs enough to get a good kick in, their grip wouldn't allow it.

Finally, Tony's head snapped back with a jerk as Calvin pulled the hair on the back of his head. The kid lost his grip on Genie's leg, and the big man pulled his leg back and kicked out at Simon, offering a weak kick to the kid's shoulder that did little to help.

He pulled back once more, further this time, lifted his heel, and connected with Simon's face. There was a loud smack, and then he was gone, headfirst out the door, with only his thigh and one arm holding on for dear life.

For the next few seconds, nobody moved. Thoughts were being processed, decisions being made. Then a scream that trumped any either man had ever heard before, even in the war, came from Simon's mouth as the train sucked him under, followed by what might have been the muffled sound of bones snapping and flesh ripping, barely audible over the violent wind. Genie wondered if he'd even heard it at all, or if that was a soundtrack he was creating for a nightmare he'd never be able to let go of.

"Andy!" Tony—if that really was his name—grabbed Genie's

knife, then gripped the side of the open door, white-knuckling the thing and leaning out, screaming into the wind.

The two old men watched him in shock. Genie fought back tears—an unrelenting guilt swam through his mind like a maggot, tunneling its way through every safe space, tainting him with self-condemnation. Memories from the war were bad enough, years of tortuous hell as he dealt with the impact the war had made. But this was on a different level. He'd just killed a boy. And this was no battlefield on foreign land. This was in the land of milk and honey, the home of the brave. Midwest America, where baseballs cut through the sky on their way to an open mitt, and kids that were Simon's (Andy's) age rode on bicycles, or in new-to-them cars with crisp licenses in their wallets, a whole life ahead of them.

"Andy!" the boy screamed again.

As though sensing his friend's guilty conscience, Calvin said, "You had to Genie. Wasn't any other way."

But Genie just stared at the space where the boy once sat, where his friend now sobbed with grief at the life lost.

"He was tryin' to kill you, Genie." Calvin shook his friend—one hand on his leg (the murder weapon) and the other on his arm.

Lightning flashed spasmodically, filling the car with the brilliance of an operating room, and it was within that seizure of flashes that Calvin saw what Genie had already forgotten: the figure in the far end of the car, only Calvin saw every unmistakable detail—a young, naked girl with her legs spread wide, knees bent. She stared back at Calvin with lifeless eyes.

While "Tony" mourned the loss of his friend at the open door—knife in hand—Calvin stood and, without warning, shoved the kid into the storm.

"Cal!" Genie swung his legs under him and crawled to the doorway, grabbing hold of the door and looking out, searching for the boy. But the stormy night had eaten any sign of him. "God almighty, Cal . . . what have we done?"

But Calvin was already at the far end of the car, striking match after match until one lit, covering the girl in a haunting orange glow. Calvin looked down at her, the bruises on her wrists, the scratches on her neck, and the pool of semen leaking from between her legs.

"Justice . . . that's what we done."

CHAPTER 10

GENIE SUPPORTED HIMSELF with one trembling hand on the train-car wall and walked on shaky legs toward Calvin and the body. Outside, the storm had calmed, almost as though it'd been appeased by the sacrifice of two teenagers.

Calvin lit another match. He'd seen enough, but Genie hadn't. Calvin knew Genie needed something to kill the guilt of kicking the kid, or it'd haunt him forever.

"Good God, Cal." His voice was a rusty hinge, the last bit of air from a leaky tire. "They do this, ya think?"

"No doubt in my mind. They crept from these same shadows, acting strange as a three-eyed cat. Didn't want us finding 'em out. That's why they were trying to throw you off. And I was next."

"They was just babies. What could have driven them outta their minds like that?" Genie dropped to his knees and bowed his head, like he was offering a quick prayer for the girl. "Just babies . . . "

Calvin bowed his head too but kept his eyes open, staring at the small diamond ring on the girl's bluing pinky, at the Daddy Long Legs making its steady way across her cold cheek.

"The world's a cesspool," he said. "But it's birthing demons now. Not just raising 'em. They're gettin' younger and younger. Much more crafty, better costumes."

Other than the clang of the tracks, the car was silent. But the echo of screams in the wind still lingered.

"We can't stick around here, Genie. Next stop, we're gone. They find us in here with her, we got too much against us. Homeless bums and smellin' like it. And no offense, but you bring a whole other level of suspect to the scenario. Civil rights ain't recognized by some. I mean . . . I know we ain't in the Deep South, but who knows which towns still have a lynchin' tree?"

"Tell me I ain't no murderer, Cal." Genie's eyes bulged with water.

"You're a damn hero, Eugene MacDowell. Who knows if this was the first time those bastards did this? And I doubt it'd have been the last. A hero. Besides . . . if anyone's a murderer, it's me. I pushed that kid while his back was turned and he was sobbing. But I'll never shed a tear for that shit stain. Not ever."

Genie just shook his head, his face contorted like he'd smelled something bad.

Both men gave the girl one last glimpse, assuring that her face would never leave the darkest corners of their minds, then went back to where they'd sat before hell reared its ugly head.

As they sat in the clanging silence, Genie continued to struggle, debating on whether or not he should feel the guilt that threatened to smother him. Then he would think of the girl, leaking sin only twenty feet away. They had to have done this. Her skin was still porcelain-like, though bluing, a necklace of small bruises around her thin throat. Her beautiful face was frozen, not sunken. Not yet.

Calvin went to his duffel and pulled the drawstring, rummaged in the deep throat of the thing, and removed one of his shirts—a large button-down that was once dark blue, now just wrinkles and thinning thread. He went back to the girl and draped it over her small body. His eyes twinkled like jewels when the moon pointed out the tears in them.

"I cover you out of dignity, out of respect and out of love, from a stranger who wishes he'd been here sooner. Fly on, little angel."

Calvin nodded and looked to his friend, but Genie was somewhere else, lost in his head, his mind going back to the question Calvin had asked just before the storm:

"Would you have done it?"

"Killed him? If it meant us or him."

"Hell, I don't know that I've got it in me anymore, Genie. If it came down to it."

He was hoping they'd never have to find out. But they had.

CHAPTER 11

ONLY A FEW MINUTES passed before the train began to slow. The rain had stopped, and the wind calmed to less than a whisper. The air reeked of worms, earth, and old wood. If it was midday, the sun would shine, unhindered. It's as though the hand of God turned a moldy page in an old dusty book. Motes of light bobbed in the darkness. Fireflies. Odd for this time of year as well as time of night. But seeing them brought back that feeling from long, long ago, when as children they ran through high grass, catching the insects in canning jars. Not realizing that to capture the light was to kill it. The earliest life lesson. The men just sat on the edge of the doorway and watched the lightning bugs dance in the cool night air above the field as the train crept.

The screech of metal on metal and the sudden lurch informed them the train was stopping altogether.

"You think they saw them boys fall out?" Genie half-gasped when asking. His wet eyes were wide and wild.

"Maybe, maybe not. But we ain't waiting around to see. Grab your suitcase and let's get."

Calvin hopped down first and, after a quick scan of the train line for bulls or cops or anyone, reached up to help his friend. "Come on, old man."

With a sore hamstring, Genie grabbed Calvin's hand and jumped down, knees buckling but not betraying him. He looked around and back into the empty car. The thin arm of moonlight that managed to make it in shined on the covered body of the girl, her alabaster legs sticking out from under the old, worn shirt that was her death shroud. "I'm sorry, child."

The two jogged down the slope to the waiting gulley that ran along the tracks, drowned in inches of rain.

"Feet are soaked." Calvin half chuckled. Genie stayed quiet, just looking ahead and trudging through the wet grass and weeds.

"You okay?" Calvin clamped a hand on his friend's shoulder, stopping his stride and forcing the burlier man to turn and face him.

"I'm as good as a man who killed a kid can be," Genie snapped and resumed his stride. Calvin sighed and followed. By the time they reached the end of the ditch, they heard the sound of the train's slow return to its journey and assumed the grisly cargo in the belly of it went undiscovered.

CHAPTER 12

EVEN WITH ONLY the feeble fingers of moonlight to illuminate the view, the two men stood on the knoll and looked down at the small town nestled in the valley.

Calvin smiled, and it was genuine, not just for Genie's sake. He seemed to have already moved on, where Genie struggled. "We can't hold onto it, Genie. Leave it back there. Wasn't nothing could be done. We've both killed before. It doesn't matter that this ain't Germany. It was war inside that car, and those were evil kids. Not in their right minds . . . mighta been drugs, mighta just been crazy. Matters none. It was war. Meditate on that and that only. You hear?"

Genie took a deep breath and nodded.

Calvin looked at his friend. "We're living what few days we got left, and dammit, I'll not let some scum of the earth take them from me. We were doin' good. We *did* good."

Genie nodded again and wiped his face, stood up straight, and fixed his posture.

Calvin looked back toward the valley. "Looks like it slid right off a postcard, don't it?"

The scene before them was some Norman Rockwellian Mayberry wet dream shit for sure. Calvin had his hands on his hips, his chest thrust out, as he drew in the fresh night air. Genie tried to mimic his friend, but all it did was court a coughing fit that left his lips tingling and rimmed red. He wiped them on the back of a weathered hand, then discreetly on his pant leg.

"I believe the word would be quaint, maybe even picturesque." Genie spoke, and it was sandpapery. He coughed once more and smiled at his friend. Calvin smiled back but only with his mouth.

"I never believed in destiny, but I tell you, I'm feeling a pull here and now that's telling me to drop anchor. That these old bones are home."

"We're always home, Cal . . . Home is where you lay your head, wherever you have a friend, and wherever the sun warms you."

"How is it you never made a mint writing greeting cards? You fart and a platitude falls out your ass."

"Only the shitty ones."

The men spilled a quiet chuckle and kept their gaze on the town, won over by its beauty and quiet charm, yet both seemingly terrified to descend into it, as though their intrusion would bring a blight of some sort. They took a few steps before stopping near the sign erected alongside the paved road. *Welcome to Crownover*, it offered. *Small in stature, big in heart*, loped beneath it in tilted script.

They paused a moment and scanned their surroundings, searching for trees where the bright moon's light didn't much break through. Calvin pointed down a path that was flattened through the tall grass and weeds and into a small forest of trees and wild brush.

"Looks like a fine motel over in those woods. Vacancy sign and all." Calvin smiled at his silliness, and Genie responded with a nod, feeling worn and a little sleepy.

They made their way to the end of the path and navigated the scant field of stones it opened into, which narrowed and withered until it became the trail again. A few minutes later, the path became nothing but a tight squeeze through encompassing brambles, dotted with bright berries that shone like eyes in the night.

"Doin' all right?" Calvin said as he jogged a few steps to catch up to his friend.

"Tired is all. Happens when a fella gets to an age, ya know."

"Oh, I know that song. All the damn words."

They followed the brush until the path became a line of bare dirt in unkempt weeds and grasses. Genie stretched, allowing old muscles to pull and groan. He winced slightly where the boy had plucked the string behind his knee, then pointed at the swell of a hill, yards ahead, where the bones of a small building lay, leaning against the rising mound of earth and vegetation. The roof had caved in the middle, but on either side of the rend was shelter. The walls all stood, the concrete blocks used, mottled with moss and faded paint.

They cautiously investigated the property. There were a couple of empty barrels beside the doorless entryway. The door that had once been there was long rotted into the ground, the rusted knob winking like a tarnished crown in the moonlight.

Calvin picked up a long branch and swatted the weeds that hedged the building, scaring out what sounded like a mouse, maybe a chipmunk. He looked at his friend and shrugged. "All clear," he said and dropped the stick to the ground.

Genie ducked under the hanging tendrils of vine and branch that obscured the top of the doorway. He took a breath and grimaced slightly. The odor of urine was there, faded but definitely present. There was an old couch against the wall, its days of seating folks long gone. Springs poked through rotting fabric like bones, and mold dotted it like liver spots on a dying man's hands.

"You can have the couch," Genie deadpanned and pointed.

Calvin grinned and shook his head. "I think the floor will do me fine, thanks."

"Same. This spot near the door might be best. Not many stones, it's under the roof, and we can tamp down the wild grass, might be close to soft on our backs."

They took off their coats and laid them on the ground, then slowly, and not quietly, knelt and laid out on their beds. Calvin put his arms behind his head and stared into the darkness above. Genie, on his side, gazed out the doorway into the thick arm of dark. It took no time before the steady ground and cushion of the grass pulled his eyes closed, and sleep came for them both quickly.

⁂⁂⁂

"Calvin . . . " Genie's voice was a gunshot in the envelope of quiet.

Calvin opened his eyes and sighed through his nose. They hadn't been asleep for more than twenty minutes. "Yeah?" Careful not to let his voice betray his annoyance.

"We been home now, what, thirty-five years?"

Calvin drew a deep breath and pulled himself up to sit back against the cool stones of the wall. *Here we go,* he thought. "My tour ended in '44 . . . I was about to turn twenty-six . . . yours a few months after, so yeah, about that."

"You still think about it? Over there, I mean?"

"Every day . . . " Calvin sat up higher and scooched closer to his friend. These were the conversations that called for more than a friendly voice and warm eye contact. They sometimes required a hug or a gentle hand on a shaking shoulder.

34

"Same." Genie sat up into what little moonlight spilled through the door. It made the thinning hair from his head look like steel wool on a peach. He rummaged through his coat pocket, and his hand returned with a cigarette, a longish butt retrieved from the ground. Genie no longer smoked, except when the reminiscences got him. He lit the butt, pinched it between his fingers, and sucked whatever life he could get from it.

Calvin lit one too. He'd done good up until now. "I sometimes think I've gotten past the war. I can go days without thinking too hard about things. The things we've seen . . . things we've done. Then a day will come where it knocks my dick in the dirt and it's all I can think about. It's normal, brother. As normal as can be for a man killin' other men far away from home can hope to be."

Calvin shimmied closer still and laid a hand on his friend's broad shoulder.

Genie smiled at him with wet eyes and nodded. "I know," was all he said. He finished the cigarette and flicked it out into the night.

Calvin forced a smile himself. "What's got you this time, Genie?"

Genie's eyes were wide and the moon in them bright. "Same as always . . . the blown-apart boy."

"Tell me again." Calvin squeezed his friend's arm, allowing Genie the armor of a whispered voice.

"You know the story . . . "

"I do. But I know it helps. I think each time you share, its hold on you weakens and dries up. Maybe one day it'll flake away, like the scales from Paul's eyes." He squeezed taut muscle with aching fingers and forced the smile to remain.

"I wasn't even supposed to be there with 'em . . . bein' colored and all. But . . . well, you know how that went down. The ins and outs of it."

Calvin nodded.

"We was leaving the village." Genie gave an unsteady laugh. "I can't even remember the name of it . . . but that boy, I'll never forget him. Private Hartmann . . . Matthew. Never even talked to the kid before that day. We were walking along, guard down, as the area had already been evacuated. We was just coming up on a bakery, a tiny little place with the door open. And the smell of bread was thick and just hung there. You know how it can just hang there when you're hungry."

"I do." Calvin looked into his friend's eyes and saw they were far away, like looking into the wrong end of a pair of binoculars.

"It was a near distraction, as hungry as we were. You'd think I would hate the smell of yeast to this day, on account of what happened. But I don't, Cal. Despite what happened, I can down a whole loaf and thank the good Lord with every bite."

Calvin said nothing, just nodded and held on, ready to pull him back to the present when the time came.

"Hartmann was first in line. Behind him, Goodfellow, then I think Murphy, then Shea. I was off to the side like . . . I was paranoid, Cal. Declared safe or not, I didn't trust it . . . and outta nowhere come this boom that shook everything—the ground, the men . . . shit, everything. I pulled myself back up and checked the men. They was all fine . . . 'cept Hartmann . . . " Genie's voice cracked like the surface of a pond in early spring. His mouth worked to allow the rest of the words, but they were skittish and stubborn like field calves.

"What happened to him?" Calvin whispered.

"He . . . he just wasn't all there anymore. I couldn't tell which parts, between the smoke and the dust and the blood . . . and the screaming . . . I just knew . . . he wasn't the same."

Calvin caressed the trembling shoulder.

"Goodfellow and I ran to him, and I tried to pull him up but stopped when Goodfellow hollered he was comin' in half. I . . . I . . . My God, Calvin, he was splitting in the middle. He slipped from my arms and hit the ground, like a fish slappin' in the bottom of a boat. Goodfellow just sat there, moon-eyed and crying. Murphy was throwing up in the gutter, and Shea just stared up at the sky. I was kneelin' there patting this poor boy's head and telling him he'd be okay. I . . . I was lyin' to him. He weren't talking, but his eyes were moving. He was crying. His brain hadn't gotten the directive he was dead yet." Genie's words splintered into sobs, and he put his head so far down his chin rested on his chest.

Calvin leaned in and brought an arm around his big friend and squeezed as hard as he could. Bringing the bigger man close enough that his lips touched the spot on his head where the hair was thin. He felt Genie shudder as the sobs came.

"You couldn't have done nothing, Genie. And you never lied to that boy. He *was* okay. His sufferin' was over. He was released. Free and clear."

Genie's sobs grew quieter, and he slowly calmed. He turned and looked into Calvin's eyes. "You really believe that?"

"I well and truly do. There'll be no marks against you for that, my friend. No marks on your slate."

Genie laid back down and put his arm across his wet eyes, as Calvin crawled back to his makeshift bed and got situated for more sleep.

"We can maybe get a few hours before daylight," Calvin mumbled, then smiled at the quiet from Genie's side of the room. The big man must have nodded off already. Calvin turned onto his side and stared out the doorway into the darkness beyond. He felt his lids droop, and his breathing slowed as he relaxed.

His eyes were about to close for the night when he heard Genie's sleep-slurred voice float above him.

"I got a mark on it now though. My slate has a stain for sure."

Calvin rolled over and stretched his neck to look at his friend, still lying across the floor, still hiding his eyes with his arm. Genie said nothing, and the night rolled on.

CHAPTER 13

IN GENIE'S DREAM, he had a home. A modest two-bedroom house with walls that resembled notebook paper—faded horizontal lines, light blue. The house smelled of fried potatoes, onion, and pepper. Louise stood at the stove with spatula in hand, her hair draped in large curls over her shoulders, the smile on her face filled with the sun. Her mouth moved, but no words came out. It seemed to Genie he didn't need to hear them. He knew every word already, the same words she'd said so many times before. About their blessings, their love for one another, and the art of taking nothing for granted—something Genie learned from her, and it made life that much easier to bear when the storms came.

A foot to his shoulder woke the aging man. He opened his eyes, and a bright light threw them shut again.

"Rise and shine, nigger," a voice said. The voice was stern, authoritative, and sure. "I said get up!"

Genie shielded his eyes and looked down at the shiny shoes that'd prodded him. Had to be a lawman's shoes, or someone with a penchant for wearing their Sunday's best in the wee hours.

"Uhh . . . Cal?" Genie called out, pushing to his feet. Elbows and knees popped like gravel under truck tires.

"You and sleeping beauty here are trespassing," the voice said.

Finally, Calvin stirred, looked up. "Ahh hell. Here we go." Genie offered him a hand, helped him to his feet.

When the light turned on Calvin, Genie could see the figure was indeed a lawman. Cap on his head, gun at his side, toothpick in mouth. "Just napping for the night, then we was on our way, Officer."

The officer stared at the men, eyeing them up and down like a teen scoping a centerfold. "You two look like shit." The toothpick in his teeth bounced like a divining rod. He sighed, more of a heavy breath through his nose. "Listen . . . this is a small town. A nice town. And I'm the one who keeps it that way by shooin' the riff-raff and keepin' the trash picked up. And in your case, the roaches." He paused and spat the toothpick into the shadows near the doorway. "You aren't from around here, are ya?"

"Sir . . . uh, Officer. My name's Eugene. This here's my friend Calvin. I assure you we was moving on once the sun poked up. We just needed rest. We're not in the habit of causing trouble. Just a couple of old fellas."

"A couple of veterans," Calvin said. It was a line he used once before, thinking it'd win them points. He hated using it, made him feel cheap, exploitative.

The cop sighed again, louder this time, and let the moment stretch, grow pregnant and threaten to purge, before he spoke again.

"Here's what we're doing, boys. I'm gonna give you two minutes . . . That's one more than I should give, because you're old. Two minutes to dust yourselves off and get your shit together. Then we're going to town, where you'll get all the rest you need in the holding cell. Once the day cracks open, I'll give you a ride down the end of Main. That leads into Harbrich. You can be their problem from here on out."

"You're takin' us in for sleepin' in this shithole shed?" Calvin said, which caught the attention of Genie's elbow.

"I'm takin' you in cuz you're trespassing, and I'm willing to bet we search hard enough, you probably left some defecate around here too. That's against the law. Now, we can stay here and look for your turd so I can push your nose in it, or we can head into town and you can get them forty winks, then make doody in a proper receptacle."

Calvin grabbed his duffel like it was a fat snake that was apt to slither off, and Genie quietly mumbled, "Bullshit," then went for his battered case.

The policeman shined his light on the rough trail back to the road. "All right. Let's move."

The trio walked out of the building and into the crisp air of the night, the shadows and slight breeze dancing for them. The sound of their feet on the dirty stones and twigs the only noise there was, as they followed the bouncing beam of the officer's flashlight. Genie felt a hard knot in his stomach. This was the kind of thing that happened to them in the city. They didn't expect that scourge to follow them here, this far away from subways, alley cats, and cardboard beds.

"Slight hill coming up, downward. You'll see my car by the gulley. Don't try anything. I'm too tired to run but ain't too lazy to shoot."

"To shoot—?" Calvin started, but Genie ended it with a quick slap to his friend's arm.

"We won't try nothing, Officer," Genie said through his teeth, a squinty glare at his friend.

"Mallon. Officer Mallon." The cop's voice was even and smooth.

They walked the rest of the way down to the waiting car in relative silence, wondering if this was the end of their plight. If they'd been silly for trying it in the first place.

Officer Mallon held the rear door open like a limo driver, waiting for the two to duck their heads and scootch in. "No charges, but you two have got to know the way things are run around here." He said it like it was a favor and they should be thankful.

As the cop shut the door and walked around to the driver's side, Genie whispered, "You shit in them woods?"

"Nope. Only cuz I was too tired. But you'd best believe I'm leavin' one in the station. Won't flush it, either."

Genie smiled. It was a real one. "Do me a favor, hold it off until we're about to leave."

"'Course," Calvin said.

Officer Mallon opened the door, got in, slammed it shut. "As I was saying, we don't allow bums around here. That's the problem with New York City, Los Angeles, Chicago. They let folks like you shit where you sleep. Fucks the whole town up. Next thing you know, Jane Doe gets raped on her way home from school, and people are steppin' on needles and broken glass on their morning jog, air reekin' of piss and B.O. No way in hell I'll let Crownover turn to that." He put his arm on the back of the seat, turned around to face the men through the mesh that separated them, looked straight at Genie. "Besides, you're a little dark for this town."

Neither man said a word. They learned a long time ago that some arguments weren't worth chasing, especially when it came to folks who thought they could read the whole book by looking at the cover from across a room.

"I'll see to it you get a meal for your trek outta here in the a.m. Now, if you'll excuse me . . . " He swung back around and fiddled with the radio until Paul Harvey's voice filled the tobacco-tainted car: *"And on the eighth day, God looked down on his planned paradise and said, 'I need a caretaker.' So God made a farmer."*

The two listened to Harvey as he went on about welfare and the national debt, bad parenting, radicals, and the moral decay of America. Every once in a while, Officer Mallon would spit a "That's what I'm talkin' about," or "Exactly!" or "You're preaching to the choir, brother."

Genie listened and couldn't help but wonder, not for the first time, how so many folks could get it so desperately wrong while trying to get it right.

Calvin watched out his window as the small town unspooled and rolled by like a flickering filmstrip.

"Damn straight!" Mallon hooted from the front seat, smacking the dash as punctuation.

CHAPTER 14

GENIE WOKE, the wheeze of air beneath the thin, vinyl mattress a stranger to him. He rolled over and looked at the ceiling. Hairline cracks sprouted from the bland light fixture like spider legs.

"You finally awake, fair princess?"

Genie started and sat upright fast enough to make his head swim a little. He noted the bars first. And then his suitcase on the floor by the door with the lock on it. The door, not fully closed or latched. His vision focused, and he saw Calvin sitting at the side of a desk, a cup of coffee steaming by his right hand, his left poised above a game board, getting ready to cast a roll of dice.

"Mornin'," his friend said and tilted a small card enough for him to see what it said before laughing. *Get out of jail free.*

"Who plays Monopoly in jail at . . . What time is it anyway?" Genie stood and stretched, his muscles cursing him.

"We do. And it's almost ten. Wayne and I got bored waiting on you, so we started without."

"Appreciate that, I guess. Who's Wayne?" Genie took slow steps to make his way out of the cell to the desk, where an empty chair waited for him. "Don't suppose there's more coffee."

"Wayne is the deputy. He's a little nicer than Officer Doody from this morning."

At the juvenile nickname, Genie snorted and shook his head.

"There might be." Deputy Jeremy Wayne walked out of a door marked restroom, then grabbed the pot of coffee from the warmer. He poured some of its contents into one of the mugs that were stacked beside it. "Sugar I can offer. Cream, I cannot."

"That'll do, thank you." Genie took the mug and loudly sipped the brew. After a few long minutes, his brain cleared, and the caffeine began to punch and pull his nerves into working. Synapses

42

firing properly. "I suppose once you guys are done with your game, we'll move on out. I apologize for muddying your carpet of a town here."

"Calvin told me your whole sad stories. Still can't have you sleeping in the woods or tramping it up and down Main Street. But Mallon can be harsh, much harsher than necessary. He watches too much TV and doesn't laugh enough." The deputy put a finger in the air. "I do have an idea of what I can maybe do. Soon as you gulp that cuppa sludge there, you fellas wash up and we'll head over to the church."

Genie looked at Calvin with wide eyes, and his friend shrugged. They finished their coffee and took time cleaning up. Deputy Wayne whistled the same tune no less than three times while they washed their faces and changed into fresh clothes pulled from their luggage.

As Genie maneuvered the last button on his shirt, he leaned over to his friend and whispered, "You still gonna pinch one off?"

Calvin shook his head. "Nah. I'll hold it. Maybe we'll get lucky and find ourselves near Mallon's lawn."

CHAPTER 15

THE POLICE STATION sat on a hill, overlooking all of downtown Crownover and patches of trees camouflaging suburban areas, while a mountain range hung back and above, an armless elder god, majestic in looming bulk. Neither of the men had ever seen a range quite like this. Equal parts crag and foliage—towering trees of various types like spiky scales on a giant beast, yet from this distance they were uniform, almost smooth in appearance, a gray undercoat in a massive painting.

"Gorgeous," Genie said as the two stood with ratty suitcase and duffel in hand. He felt that exciting fear that came with starting over in a town you'd never been to, no one having seen your face before, and with no guarantee that things would work how you'd like. It brought back even more of that youthful spirit that'd teased him when they first set off.

"God's own canvas," Calvin said, his voice barely above a whisper.

"Speaking of God, you fellas have a meeting at his house." Deputy Wayne stood next to them, seemingly prideful in showing off his town.

To Genie, the words almost sounded like the preface to a bullet in the head from a dirty cop. While the deputy seemed to be one of the good ones, Genie still didn't have reason to trust the man just yet. It'd take more than a game of Monopoly and a cup of coffee to do that.

The three got in the patrol car. It didn't reek of cigarettes and sweat the way Mallon's did. This vehicle smelled new, with a hint of something sweet. Genie figured that was donuts, long-eaten glaze and powdered sugar that hung in the air like ghosts, freed on uneventful mornings while sitting in a parking lot, waiting for crime to rear its head.

The mesh between the seats, along with the locked doors,

kicked Genie's paranoia up a notch. He wanted to know more about Deputy Wayne and his intentions with them. "So, you got a good cop, bad cop thing goin' on with you and Mallon?"

The deputy drove with one hand on the wheel, the other adjusting the visor against the morning sun. "It's not the way we put it together. Just the way it is."

"What's up Mallon's ass, anyway?" Calvin chimed in.

"Pride. No woman." At that, something somber flitted across Wayne's face, quick as a blink, then he continued, "That's a big part of it."

"Hell of a lot more than that," Calvin said.

"He never married, but he had a gal once, wasn't really his to have. That ended badly. Now he lives in the same house he was born in. Lived there with his sister until she died a few years back." Wayne's smile wilted while he spoke, but he pulled it tight again and went on.

"Anyway, Mallon's not exactly the joyous type."

"Having no wife doesn't seem to cover all his thorns," Calvin said. "Way he made it sound, we're the plague. Made sure to point out Genie here's the *black* plague. This whole town see color that way, or just a wart in the bunch?"

Deputy Wayne caught Genie's eyes in the rearview, gave a sympathetic look. "Hmm . . . Mallon played that card, did he? Well . . . I'd be lying if I told you he's the only one, but there ain't many. I think you'll find the hospitality in Crownover looks past skin and into the heart. Lots of God-fearin' folks here."

"I think it should be noted," Genie said. "If you're taking us somewhere here in town, Mallon also made it clear we was to close the door behind us. Mentioned something about one town over."

"Don't you worry about Sheriff Mallon. I may just be a deputy, but I got a little pull. Now, a bit about where I'm taking you. I made a phone call this morning, and if you're up for it, I may have found you work, as well as room and board."

"Yep . . . this sounds more and more like a trap," Genie half joked.

The deputy chuckled. "I think after meeting Mr. Rosem you'll find yourself at ease."

The two friends traded glances, each of them hidden behind a wall they weren't ready to tear down just yet.

***

The patrol car pulled into a cemetery, its tenants a mixed bunch. Some of the tombstones had lost their engravings years ago, packed with moss and dirt, while the rest looked as new as last week. Granite sparkled in the morning sun like diamonds. The entryway went through a wrought-iron gate, then made a fork. The right started up a hill, and the left trailed off behind a row of pines. They took the right.

The road hugged the hill a ways until it went straight up, then flattened, where a building that had the makings of an office sat. A brick-and-granite sign resting heavy out front read *Kimball Pines Cemetery.*

"Don't look much like a church," Calvin said, peering out the back window like a kid who expected to ride the Ferris wheel after being told he's headed to the fair.

"This here's the office." Deputy Wayne nodded at the brick building. "The church is down the other side of the hill. I guess technically it's not a church but a memorial, though a shitload of prayin' goes on in it. Important thing is, this is your HQ. The man inside holds the power of a paycheck. He strikes you as fit, you're on your way to gettin' new threads, as the kids say."

The car came to a stop, and the deputy got out, opened the back doors. The men slid out, stood, and looked around.

"I got the impression we was gonna be custodians or some such for the local congregation, but now I'm thinking otherwise. Can you fill us in?" Genie said.

"I'll leave that to Mr. Rosem." Deputy Wayne pointed toward the office. "He's just beyond those doors." The deputy got back in the running car and leaned out the window, tilting his head so the brim of his hat cut the sun from his eyes. "Good luck, fellas. And I'll be seeing you around if you stick. If you don't, I'd probably blow outta town. See . . . my thinking is, you got a job and a place to live, you're not bums. You're citizens. And no matter how mad that makes Mallon, ain't a thing he can do about it. It's a win-win. You have work, money, and a place, and Mallon is annoyed. I can't help but find amusement in that."

Wayne knocked the door of his car twice as a sendoff, then clicked it into gear and turned the vehicle around, the low front bumper coming close to clipping a listing tombstone bleached white as bone. The cruiser slowly headed back to town while Genie and Calvin made their way up the path to the building that was HQ.

CHAPTER 16

A **WOMAN**, who Genie thought was probably the secretary, sat at a desk. She was old enough to assume she might be purchasing one of the plots herself soon. Cheeks covered rosy-red, costume jewelry, and what was most likely a wig standing tall on her head, either that or some sort of magic holding a natural thick, gray nest up that high.

"Why, hello, gentlemen." She had the voice of Mickey Mouse— high-pitched and nasally, but pleasant. *With a voice like that*, Genie thought, *no way has she ever had a shot of whiskey or so much as caught some secondhand smoke.* "You must be here from the jail. Pastor Rosem is expecting you. You can go right in." She pointed a bony finger at the first door in a short hall. The door held a small sign that read *Pastor Paul Rosem.*

"Thank you, ma'am," Calvin said.

Genie nodded. "Ma'am."

The two headed to the door, which stood ajar, and knocked.

"Come on in," a voice called from the other side.

They entered single file.

A man stood up from behind a desk much bigger than the one out front.

"Mornin', boys. I'm Paul Rosem." His voice was deep and rich. Genie had no trouble at all imagining it at pulpit volume, eschewing sin and welcoming salvation. The preacher's face was sunned a deep brown and well-lined. He wore faded jeans and a flannel shirt with snaps, the sleeves rolled to just below the elbows.

Genie nodded and smiled when he replied. "Good morning yourself, Father. The secretary lady said to come on in."

"Heh. This church isn't quite big enough for a secretary. Marie is our parishioner who comes in twice a week and straightens up the mess I make, types up the Sunday bulletin. And I'm no father. Just a lowly reverend. Pastor will do, but Paul would do better."

"And we're a long way from the boy's side of the yard, Paul. Closer to grave dirt than Gerber."

The stocky man chuckled. "Of course . . . gentlemen." He held out a hand, and Genie took it, shook firmly. "Please, have a seat." He presented two cushioned chairs in front of the desk with a wave of his hand. Genie claimed one, and after Calvin offered his own hand in greeting, he claimed the other. Paul made his way around the desk and sank back into his chair. It squeaked when he swiveled forward to face them.

"I suppose the best way to start would be your names."

"I'm Eugene MacDowell. But you can call me Genie. Everyone does." He looked down at his threadbare pants, his worn-out boots, and suddenly felt a twinge of shame. Like there was nowhere in this garden he could hide.

"Calvin. Calvin Thomas. Pleased to meet you." Calvin shook Paul's hand again.

Paul smiled and backed it with twinkling eyes. He cleared his throat and then spoke. "So, the deputy tells me the two of you are looking for work."

"Yessir," Genie said, his smile back in place. "We threw our dice back in Chicago, hopped on a train to come out west, hoping we'd find something. Luck has landed us here." Genie realized right away that luck wasn't quite the word he was looking for. Luck had nothing at all to do with why they were here. They were here because some necro-rapist kids—that they happened to kill, even if by accident—left them no choice but to take the next stop.

"We'll take anything we can get at this point, Pastor Paul," Calvin said. "The deputy also mentioned room and board?"

Paul nodded, the smile he wore growing in size, and pulled his chair forward, allowing a little of the distance between him and the men to shrink. Up close they could see the numerous tiny wrinkles nested in the corners of his shining blue eyes.

"That's right. My own son, he's done this work every summer for the last five years. But he's a grown man now, off to college. It's steady work, but the labor can be tough, though I figure with two of you working that'll be less so. It can also be a sad job, if you've an empathetic heart."

"Yep." Calvin hadn't meant to speak aloud.

"Essentially, you'll be taking care of upkeep on the grounds. Mostly the lawn, weeds, trimming hedges, gathering branches and trash after storms, digging graves as needed. We get the occasional vandal, but they tend to steer clear when they know someone's living in the cottage. I often just leave the outside light on over there, and it usually does the trick."

"The room and board," Genie said. "That's here in the cemetery?"

"Yes, it is. A cute little cottage at the edge of the property." Pastor Rosem steepled his fingers.

"What's the wages?" Calvin asked the question.

"Well, technically it's a one-man job, and I'm assuming you're a package deal, so you'll have to split the pay. But you'll both have beds and will make plenty for food, as well as a little pocket money . . . assuming you're not down at Loretta's Lunchbox for every meal." The pastor chuckled, and the lines around his eyes cracked deeper. "We serve supper every night at the big church, so there's another meal you won't have to save for, as well as Sunday mornings, when the table's lined with more donuts than you can count. Potluck every other Sunday afternoon, though I'd stay away from Ms. Halverson's macaroni salad . . . but you didn't hear that from me." The pastor used air quotes when saying *macaroni salad*.

"As I mentioned, your housing will be in that little cottage at the end of the property, by the fence. Was the old parsonage back in the thirties. When they built bigger digs, that became a guest house of sorts. Rarely used, but it has all the comforts of home. A bathroom, small kitchen, two small bedrooms, and a living area. Utilities are covered by the church."

"We get a roof overhead, an honest-to-God toilet, a handful of home-cooked meals for free . . . and how much money?" This time it was Genie who broached the subject. The reverend fidgeted a little before sighing and squinting at the men.

"I can manage a hundred bucks a week, that'd be fifty a piece. And keep in mind that's under the table. It's a bit more than the budget allows, and I'm covering the difference. So please, don't disappoint me. I can see you're good men. I can see you've known hard times. And I feel God has given us both this opportunity. So, if you want it . . . "

"We're in," Calvin and Genie replied in unrehearsed unison. The three men laughed in the small room, and it floated out the screened window and down the street like a breeze.

CHAPTER 17

THE REST OF the morning was spent extensively going over their expected duties. While Kimball Pine had two riding lawnmowers, one push mower, and a new gas-powered weedwhacker available, the two men were surprised to find the graves were dug with shovels. "We've invested plenty in tools for groundskeeping, but any machinery for digging graves is something we don't see the necessity for," the pastor had said. "We like to consider ourselves a progressive town, but a good, old-fashioned spade does the trick just fine." He cut his eyes to Genie, and his lips disappeared. "Uhh . . . sorry . . . I mean shovel."

Genie nodded. "I can tell when the word means shovel and when it's being used as a weapon."

The pastor nodded back before he spoke again. "Besides, you get one of those backhoes out here, you got a mess on your hands."

Once every instruction was given, and a tour of the cottage was over, Paul left the men to settle in, reminding them dinner was at five. Without unpacking, they rested on their beds, recovering from the lack of sleep the night before. Their rooms were separated by a small hallway, making conversation from their respective rooms obtainable without raising a voice.

While they hadn't intended on falling asleep, that's the way it shook out. The beds were soft yet unyielding. Heaven, really.

CHAPTER 18

AFTER A LENGTHY NAP, Genie was up first, stirred by a coughing fit that left his mouth tasting of copper. "Lord help me," he whispered, then squinted his eyes as he made his way toward his suitcase, still sitting in the doorway where he left it. Once he placed it on the bed and sat down, he put pen to paper and wrote another note to Louise—a less-than-stellar way to mark a new life, as the words reserved for her often brought tears and were best left written after dark, where he could hide his face and sleep off the grief of missing her. He sniffed the scarf she'd made and rubbed it between his thumb and fingers, pretending she still held the other end.

Calvin stirred across the small hallway. Bedsprings squeaked as weight shifted. Genie wiped his face, put the pen in his shirt, and began to fold the letter when Calvin walked into the hallway just outside his room.

Calvin watched the hurried way Genie tried to hide the note but chose to ignore it. "I'm startin' to think one of us needs a watch," he said, rubbing the sleep from his eyes.

"A watch? What for? Time don't move any faster just 'cause your eye's on it. Besides, takes away some of that carefree spirit, don't it?"

"To hell with that. I like to know if my belly's screamin' for breakfast or lunch."

Genie looked out the window and at the bright sky. "Can't be more than an hour past noon."

"Noon? Damn . . . I guess we were catchin' up, huh?"

"We're sleepin' on clouds, my friend."

Calvin's eyes wandered in reflection. "Remember that time we were staying in the old shed? It was Fourth of July—"

"And the dogs kept us up."

"All. Night. Long. Wasn't even the fireworks. It was the damn barkin'."

"But we wouldn't leave cuz them mattresses."

"Brand new, wrapped in plastic, and stored away."

"Ain't no dogs barkin' here." Genie smiled.

"Feels like one of them too-good-to-be-true scenarios, doesn't it?"

"Well, if it's a dream, don't wake me."

"I'm gonna grab a shower. A long, steamy one." Calvin disappeared from the doorway and hummed as he made his way down the short hall.

Genie waited until he heard the door at the end of the hall close before taking out the letter once more. He touched his tongue with the tip of the pen and let it hover above the paper until he was pulled from his trance by the sound of running water and Calvin's high-pitched, celebratory laughter.

CHAPTER 19

WALKING ALONG THE GRAVESTONES, scoping out the newer plots, and wondering just how long it took to dig a hole six feet deep, Genie said, "Since we don't officially start until tomorrow, what say we go check out the neighborhood?" His freshly washed dome shined where the hair lacked on the top.

"And what of the sheriff?"

"Like the deputy said, we're citizens now, and he'd take care of it."

"Since when does a minion have pull over their master? That's all I'm sayin'."

"This sounds like something you'd say, but . . . Calvin Thomas, did you come all this way just to run with your tail between your legs?"

"That does sound like something I'd say . . . Let's get to it, then," Calvin muttered as he began to take longer strides down the hillside. Genie did the same, albeit slower. Where most folks would see a small, paved road opening into a two-way street that ran several blocks flanked by buildings and businesses, the men saw wide-open arms.

"Get some local eats?" Calvin said, stretching his right arm into the air as high as he could, trying to soothe its soreness as the hardwood floor of the train had done a number on his shoulder.

Genie nodded, but he wasn't paying particular attention. His eyes were eating up the main street of town. Not quite a town, were it nestled in a quaint European setting, more a village or a burg. The old man's lips curled into a genuine smile, one that allowed teeth to greet light and air.

"Earth to Genie." Calvin nudged his friend and snapped him from his preoccupation.

"Sorry, I was . . . It's just. Look at this. It's like it fell outta the television back in the day. Like Mayberry or wherever the hell Beaver lived."

"Quaint is the word you want, Professor." Calvin was grinning now too, his joy stemming not from the picturesque little place they'd found themselves in, but at the fact his friend seemed to be expressing contentment and legitimately so. No more blood-tinged guilt, no more missing Louise, no more sickness or flashbacks. Not in this moment.

Genie looked over at the small squat box of barnwood painted red. The long, wide counter that ran across the front and along the visible side. The few picnic tables scattered around the grass in front, all hosting napkin dispensers and red and yellow squirt bottles. He read the sign out loud to himself. "Loretta's Lunchbox." His voice cracked slightly, and his eyes brightened.

"With lunch in us and dinner at five, we'll be bloated royalty, laying our heads on an honest-to-goodness pillow, mattress springs squeakin', showing mercy on our asses."

They made their way down the sidewalk, passing folks who mostly kept their eyes elsewhere. When they did finally get a friendly nod, their posture straightened and their hearts sang a bit louder.

..*.

They sat at the table furthest from the building, almost hidden in the shade of a large tree. The slight breeze made the leaves whisper above them as they tucked into their loose meat sandwiches. Genie was savoring the slightly spiced beef and tomato sauce, while his friend was assaulting his plate of fries, drowning them in ketchup.

They scanned their surroundings as they ate, expecting to find a wall of revulsion and disdain in the faces of the other patrons, but while there were a few scowls, most paid them no mind. Calvin slid the last fry to its demise before he dabbed his lips with a napkin and dropped it onto his empty tray.

"That was good. I haven't had French fries—fresh, hot and salty-as-hell fries—in I don't know how long."

Genie nodded and spoke through a mouthful of sandwich. "I think the closest we came were the nights we managed to catch the kid at The Dolphin taking out the trash. Sometimes they were almost still warm." He wiped his mouth, then leaned back until his spine popped.

"Two beans for a sandwich that good, a heap of fries, and two colas. Not bad."

"Small-town prices, I guess. Plus, look at us, probably thought we was in need. Come that first pay day, we're getting new duds." Genie brushed his pant legs like they'd somehow clean up and the small holes would patch as long as his intentions were pure enough.

He looked around again to see if anyone was lobbing a stink eye in their direction. There was a clean-cut, young-looking man with a button-down shirt sitting with a pair of kids at a table near the street, and while it wasn't exactly stink eye, it was far from kindness. Genie felt his smile start to slip, that deep-seated shame sliding back over him like a shawl.

"Wanna get an ice cream before the rest of the sightseeing tour?" Calvin smiled big enough to show the squares of his front teeth.

"We've got three bucks left, should probably sit on it, even if dinner at the church is free. I don't wanna be seen here with my ass pokin' out of a dumpster when we're broke. Not in this town. In Chicago, it's expected. Here, we're damn unicorns."

Calvin agreed.

As they rose and dumped their trays into the barrel by the counter, Genie caught the eye of the woman manning the grill inside and nodded. "That was delicious, ma'am."

"Why, thank you. You gentlemen just passin' through?"

"I think you'll be seeing us around. You've got yourself a swell-looking town here." Genie used his strong voice. The one that walked straight and tall. He waved to the woman and jogged to catch up to Calvin, who was nearly to the corner.

The two resumed their walk around town, bellies full. Above them, the sun began to slide down the far side of the sky.

"Most definitely gettin' new clothes. We're gonna burn these rags," Genie said. "With a fresh start here, no reason to make 'em clutch their purses when we pass by. Every bit of Chicago needs to be left behind."

"Like Louise?" It was a whispering mumble, purposefully quiet so Genie wouldn't hear.

"Know what I mean, Cal?"

"We should buy tuxedos."

"Patent leather two-tone shoes."

"Like dapper sonsabitches." Genie laughed, holding back an ugly cough, then choked on it as he caught a patrol car down the street, Mallon sitting behind the wheel with his arm resting on the door. The sheriff was looking straight at them. "Well . . . shit."

Calvin followed Genie's squinting eyes. "Looks like we got ourselves a babysitter."

CHAPTER 20

TO AVOID MALLON, they took the long way home and cut through the newer plots in the cemetery. Genie caught the death date on one of the smaller stones. Same as the birth date. "Damn," he said. Calvin followed his friend's eyes to the stone, and the two had a quick moment of silence that was soon broken.

"So, you're the ones." An unpleasant voice. "Two old geezers."

The men looked behind to find a kid walking toward them who couldn't have been more than twenty-two. He wore a suede, fringed jacket and shaggy hair that hadn't seen a comb in at least a week. The glare in his eyes said he wasn't happy to see them. His words said that too.

"The new guys . . . grave slaves."

"I'm in no mood to go hittin' some kid," Genie whispered. "Not again."

"We'll try another tactic," Calvin whispered back. "Nice day, isn't it?" Calvin called out as the man continued to shorten the distance between them, in clunky steps that were anything but straight.

"Ain't never a good day in this shit town, unless you're sitting high in the trees and watching from afar, just laughing away at the nonsense," the man said back through tremulous laughter. Spittle sprayed from his mouth, and flecks of it clung to the stubble on his chin.

In that moment, Genie would have loved to shove the slums of Chicago right up his ass, make him sleep on a cardboard mattress for a month, and eat scraps from the diner. Have to use tape to hold his shoes on and bread bags over his socks to keep his feet dry.

"At least we got the sunshine." Calvin kept it going, ignoring the strange bit about being in a tree and trying to douse the spark of something bad the man was lighting.

"So . . ." The man stood within striking distance now. The reek of fermentation on his breath tainted the air. "Am I right? You work for Dad now, puttin' the kids down where they belong?" He used air quotes when he said the word *belong*.

So, this was the son off to college. They noted a slight waver in the way he stood, not full unsteady but not cat-like balance either.

"Haven't actually started, but that's the agreement. My name's Calvin." Calvin stuck his hand out. It was not received, only glared at. "This big fella here's Eugene."

After seeing the man's response to Calvin's greeting, Genie kept his hand to himself, mostly fretting it may turn into a fist, and only nodded.

"You know . . . that's my job you got." His eyes were shot through like red glass, but the pupils were black marbles eclipsing any color behind them. Genie wondered if he was on more than just booze. He'd seen those eyes before, in a few of the hippies he'd run across.

The old men stayed quiet for a minute, a minute that dragged like chains. The kid sniffed back hard and spat at them. It landed about an inch from Calvin's feet. Calvin looked up from watching it hit the grass, the smile he'd been trying to hold folding. The breath Genie blew from his nose was a boiling kettle, and the smile on the drunk boy's face seemed to falter.

"Now listen, you little pissant . . . " Calvin's voice was booming but even, disturbing in its calm.

The boy stood staring at the old men with smoldering eyes that looked as though they hadn't closed for sleep in days. Then, "Who're you calling . . . "

"You'll shut that mouth, if you're wise," Genie interjected and nodded sideways at Calvin. "He's aimin' to tell you something. And if I were you, I'd hold tight and let him. Less likely to be stitches in your future." Genie's hands had transformed into the fists he'd feared.

Calvin sneered and took a step toward the kid, who retreated in equal measure, nearly falling over his own feet. "Listen up. I don't know your story, but from what I'm told, you're a college boy now. If that ain't true, then take it up with your old man. Not us. But if it's a spankin' you want, we're ready to give it."

At that last line, Genie held back a laugh and looked off to the left, at the tall statue of a cement angel—cold gray and dappled with bird shit.

"Shut your hole, Fossil. I don't care about this job. Planting people and picking up sticks. Hell, ain't nothing to *that* . . . " He laughed, and it was an unhealthy thing that practically galloped from his throat.

The men noticed there were tears in his eyes, but Genie found he was all out of sympathy. It'd been a hard road, and this peckerhead was making it harder still. Harder to smile even when the sun gave reason to. Harder because of assholes like this, which he had hoped to God were only in Chicago. But with each new face met, it was a roll of the dice on whether or not there was a halo under the hat or a pair of pointy horns.

"That's right. I don't give a shit. I'll hide with the owls, and we'll all sit back and laugh at you, digging those holes that don't mean a thing. You geezers can have the job and all the bullshit that goes with it . . . " He cast a slightly worried glance at the church, then swiveled back to look at the men. "And let me tell you, there's plenty of bullshit . . . "

The young man turned and started walking toward the gate but hadn't gone a step before Genie clapped a big hand on his shoulder.

"Slow yourself, son. You owe us an apology for the spitting, I feel. We're all civilized adults here." Genie's eyes were squinty sharp things aimed at the kid's throat.

That's when the young man tried to throw a punch, one that was telegraphed for what seemed like years before actually being thrown.

Genie gripped the kid's smaller fist in his and squeezed until knuckles cracked, then let go, not intending to break it. Calvin grabbed his big friend and pulled him back.

"Sorry about spittin'. Now . . . leave us alone." The kid's voice was thin and ready to tear like paper. "We're outta here."

The men watched him hold his hand close to his chest before he turned once again and started walking. When the gate had squeaked closed and the young man had staggered out of sight, Genie let out the breath he'd been holding, which turned into a sequence of coughs that sounded like seals being clubbed. When the fit was over, he spit thick phlegm to the ground, quickly mashing it into the grass with his foot in case it contained blood.

"That young fella's a little off his rocker," Calvin said.

"A little? I think that boy done took the brown acid."

"What do you wager that was all about?" Calvin asked as he sat down on the edge of the angel statue's base.

"In a nutshell? Sounds like him and his old man aren't exactly the best of friends. And by the reek of his breath and the devil in his eyes, I got an idea why."

Calvin looked up at Genie and squinted an eye as the sun beamed. "You know I'm not one to back down from a fight when a fist might fix more than words can, Genie. But . . . "

"Say no more." Genie threw his hand up. "My pride got in the way. That was my knee jerkin' is all. When we get handed an opportunity like we did today, then some drunk fool comes along and tries to piss on it . . . well, I forgot to count to ten."

"I just don't want to give reason to boot us, or any grief from the sheriff. That cat ain't gonna be happy we're still in Mayberry anyhow."

"We're on the same team, my friend." Genie reached his hand out to help Calvin up. "Promise I won't squeeze." He smiled, and his teeth peeked through his lips like corn through husk.

CHAPTER 21

THE REST OF THE DAY was spent tracing the grounds, familiarizing themselves with the terrain so when tomorrow came the cogs would spin smoothly. They looked through the barn that made for a tool shed. Light pried through cracks in the wooden walls, giving visibility to the dust motes that hung in the air like fireflies. It smelled of motor oil, gasoline, and dirt and was filled with lawnmowers—both riders and push—rakes, shovels, a few toolboxes with the necessities—hammers, screwdrivers, wrenches, loose nuts and bolts. In one far corner, an old coffin sat on top of some cinder blocks, covered in dust and cobwebs.

Genie eyed the coffin and let out a sigh. "Didn't really hit me 'til now what we're dealing with here."

Calvin was rummaging through one of the toolboxes, feeling the grip of a hammer. "And what's that?"

"Death."

Calvin tossed the hammer into the toolbox. "Well, we do work in a cemetery."

Genie ran a finger along the black casket, putting a clear line through the dust on top. "I know that, but it's more than a job. It's like death's in our face now. It's one thing to hear the creak of your knees in the morning, a reminder you ain't gettin' any younger. But to walk among the dead, to make their beds. That's almost too close . . . "

"You goin' soft on me, Genie?"

Genie realized he was holding back a tear. "Maybe." He faked a chuckle and wiped his eyes, picturing the scourge in his lungs like black mold spreading, erasing the years that'd never be.

"It's just a job, old friend. We gotta keep that in mind, look straight ahead, like the folks who drive the ambulances. The hell they must see. But God bless 'em, somebody's gotta do it."

"You'd think we'd be used to it by now . . . death." Genie turned to his friend, looked him in the eyes. "But I don't think I ever will be, Cal."

Calvin walked to his friend. "It's part of life, Genie. But only the end part. Don't let it speak before then. Don't answer that tap on the shoulder, keeping you up nights, breaking your smile, stopping you from enjoying a moment, cuz worrying about death, you may as well already be in its arms."

As the two turned from the coffin, they both heard a noise that seemed to come from inside. Their eyes met each other's, wide and startled, then back to the coffin.

Genie spoke first. "You heard that, right?"

Calvin only nodded.

"A mouse . . . had to be a mouse."

Then another sound, the kind you might hear from a bathroom stall, when the occupant's bowels are filled with bad chili.

"That ain't no mouse," Calvin whispered, then quickly went to grab the hammer he'd just had in his hand.

Genie gripped the coffin lid, waiting on Calvin's signal. With hammer in hand and ready to swing, Calvin gave the okay with a quick nod. Genie took a deep breath and swallowed hard, then threw the coffin open.

Rotten air rushed forward, filling their nostrils with the scent of human feces. Gazing back at them with saucer eyes was Jimmy Rosem, hair disheveled and mouth agape.

Genie jumped and nearly slammed the lid shut. "What in God's name are you . . . ? Dammit, boy . . . " He covered his nose, as did Calvin.

"The hell you doin' in there, son?" Calvin asked.

"Hidin'. Now back on up, so I can get out."

"Hiding? In a coffin? Boy, you ain't right." Genie backed away to grab some air and give the man room.

Jimmy kept one hand on the lid, making sure it didn't come down on him, then swung his legs over the coffin's edge. "I was trying to get some sleep, then you two come in here, taking your time, jabberin' philosophy like two old ladies who'd finally read a book."

The words on Genie's tongue were harsh, but he tucked them in his cheek for later. For now, there were too many questions. "This some kinda hippy bed? Is that it? This where you used to stay when you worked for your old man?"

"Hell no. I slept in the cottage, but you two assholes are in there."

Calvin scratched his head, furrowed his brow. "You're not even going to college, are you?"

"I was, yeah. Not that it's any of your business. But I learned too much, and the professors wanted me dead, tried poisoning me more than once. They're afraid I'm gonna take over."

"Take over?"

"When you've got a mind as free as mine, it's a threat to those who go by the book. That's all I'm saying. Think on that." Jimmy poked a finger to his temple.

Genie shook his head and snickered. "Boy, you ain't got a lick of sense about you."

Jimmy tapped his temple again, ignoring the putrid aroma that enveloped him and that corner of the room. "Them cage thinkers get all worked up."

"So, your dad. He thinks you're at school, but you're here in town, sleeping in this coffin, hiding from him."

"Again. It's not your business, but yes. I sleep in this coffin." Jimmy shook his leg like he was trying to get a snake out from inside his pants. It made the stink worse.

"You shit your pants in there, Jimmy?" Calvin asked, hand over his nose.

"You geezers wouldn't leave. I got my stomach all tied in knots, waiting on you, that poison still running through me."

Calvin spotted an old towel hanging over the lip of a rusted sink on the far wall and pointed toward it. "Get yourself cleaned up. Genie and I got a few things to talk about . . . and throw that towel the hell away when you're done." He walked outside. Genie followed.

Calvin put his hands on his hips and sighed. "Well?"

"That kid's either tripping his brains out or he done lost his mind from it a long time ago. Either way, we're in a position I thought we'd never be. This kid is homeless, Cal."

Calvin sighed again. "Maybe, but not exactly. I mean . . . he's got family. Hell, his dad's a pastor. How's a man like that gonna take in two strangers but turn his own son away? The kid's probably just stubborn, don't wanna follow Dad's rules. Like no drugs in the house."

"And if his old man won't have him, we gonna tell him to hit the road too? We ain't like that."

"That coffin's still a better bed than we've had in years, grim or not."

"So let him have the shed until we find out his story?"

"Won't hurt us none."

The two walked back into the large shed, but Jimmy wasn't there, only the smell of him.

Genie pointed to the window. It was open. "Musta booked it."

They hustled to the window and saw Jimmy, already fifty yards away and running with the strangest gait they'd ever seen, shaking one leg, then the other, doing his best to empty his pants of the mess he'd made.

CHAPTER 22

THE FIRST FEW days of work were uneventful. No sign of Jimmy or the sheriff. Genie had done his best to clean out the coffin in case the man returned, looking for a place to lay his head. He'd scrubbed it down, sprayed it with Lysol, and laid a blanket over the stained satin, even brought out an old pillow he'd found in a closet in the cottage.

Now, Genie stood in the doorway of the small home he shared with Calvin and watched the sun turn the dew to a thin carpet of fog over the ground. He held a mug in his hands and let the steam from the coffee touch his face like fingers. He breathed through his nose, and besides the earthy aroma of his drink, he smelled clean air laced with the scents of cut grass and wet earth. It was sweet and strong. He felt his lips arrange a smile and allowed it.

"What's going on out there?" Calvin spoke from behind.

Genie didn't turn to see but heard the scuffing shuffle of the other man's feet on the floorboards. "Just beauty. I musta seen me a million mornings in the city. They were smeared with smoke and strewn over with garbage. Ripped open by car horns and always bleedin' noise. But this here . . . this is magic. Even while peppered with tombstones." He swallowed the rest of his coffee and ducked back inside, leaving the door open.

"You turning into a hippie?" Calvin stood at the counter and poured the remainder of the coffee into his own mug.

"Just saying it's a miracle at work. Look out the door at the horizon. The sun and earth dancing like that. I ain't saying I wanna smoke dope and dance with a damn tambourine."

They held one another's gaze like duelists before Calvin chuckled and leaned forward, allowing the coffee that dribbled from his laughing mouth an easy trip back to the cup.

Genie grinned, shook his head, and set his mug on the table, then walked to the short hallway between their rooms. "I suspect we better head out. See what work awaits us."

Calvin talked back, louder to be heard from the kitchen. "I know this sounds terrible, but I almost wish someone'd pass so we got something to do besides picking up sticks. Two days of cuttin' and pullin' weeds—"

"Count your blessings, friend," Genie interrupted.

"Last I checked, mornings are for bitching."

"I'm just sayin', don't forget about the cardboard box you came from."

"Touché."

Calvin had just set his mug in the sink when Genie came back into the room. He had his boots in hand—a new pair Rosem had given him, had said he never wore them because he didn't like the way they fit.

Genie sat down, tied the laces on the new boots, and stood up. He peered out the window that faced the back corner of the cemetery, nearest the wall and behind the trees by the fence. He leaned forward and squinted as his nose almost touched the window glass.

"Calvin. If we got nothing else to do, I think we oughta investigate the far corner over there." His finger touched the glass, and he etched a smiley face into the grimy thing. "The grave closest to the wall. Looks like a fresh one, but the cleanup is shoddy." Genie straightened himself and turned away from the window. "Though first I suggest you get some pants on."

"You sure?" Calvin was grinning.

"Fairly," Genie said as he stepped out onto the stoop and pulled the door closed. He stared at the morning sun and felt its warmth, and that was how he waited for the next fifteen minutes.

··*

The two men stared down at the grave. It was fresh enough to where the headstone still hadn't been placed, but the dirt thrown about was what caught Genie's attention. There was no neatly flattened surface. No fertilizer down or grass seed. Where it should be flat, the ground was concave, and dirt was scattered haphazardly on surrounding graves.

"Now, either the digger before us had shit for brains, or this here was done post-mortem. Good eye, Genie."

"Graverobbers?" Genie scratched at his unruly beard.

"Not sure about that, but vandals at least."

"Could be Rosem's boy."

"Framin' us?"

"Could be. Or he coulda just been . . . Hell, I don't know what he'd be doin'. That boy's got a screw loose."

Calvin scanned that side of the cemetery, as far as he could see. "Ain't no light over here at night. No moon getting through these trees here, and them lights ain't reaching all the way over here from the street. This is the darkest part of the yard. Probably why they chose it."

Genie shook his head. "I'd agree if it weren't for this." He leaned down and pulled a small card from a dirty wreath of flowers laying on the ground. He read it aloud: "*Our precious little Lily. See you in Heaven.* It's got death dates on it. Was just last week."

"Guess that settles it. Fresh grave." Calvin stared at the wreath, and the corners of his mouth turned, as the words came out, "Ain't nothing sadder than a child's grave."

Genie squinted into the sun and wiped his forehead with the sleeve of his flannel shirt.

Calvin regretted his choice of words. It was all Genie needed was to have the weight of grief on him again. "Course . . . Death is freedom. Absolute freedom." Another poor choice. But he'd tried.

Genie turned and walked to the edge of the tree line where the fence began. His fingers went to his shirt pocket, to the paper that lived there, folded into a well-worn square. "Freedom is all anyone deserves, some just ain't wise enough to know it."

Calvin nodded behind him.

The scene, the mussed grave, the subject of dying. The hopeful glee they'd felt earlier all but evaporated. The men stood and stared at the scattered sod, until Calvin broke away and went to the shed for the shovels and a rake, while Genie grabbed a faded red wheelbarrow and pushed it toward Lily's grave.

"I'm reminded of that man they caught in Wisconsin," Genie said. "Robbin' the graves of women, taking their lady bits an' makin' jewelry out of 'em and whatnot."

"That's some morbid arts and crafts right there."

"Only reminded of it. I don't really think this town has that kinda evil in its walls. Hell, for all we know, some younguns came by with spoons and Matchbox cars, building a town right atop little Lily here."

"If it weren't such a mess, I'd call that the most logical explanation we've got."

Genie stared at the concave burial site, the dirt tossed about, then began to carefully shovel it back where it belonged. With the tools they'd brought, within the hour they'd flattened the young girl's resting place until it was level enough to pour cement.

"When it comes to diggin', I'd rather not know their age." Genie leaned an arm on the shovel. "I'd like to pretend each hole dug is for those who lived well past their prime, having milked the hell out of life."

Calvin gently placed the wreath back on the flattened grave. "Let's start with Lily, then. Sweet Lily, she was a little old lady who brought the donuts to church meetings."

Genie chuckled. "She loved game shows and gossip and made homemade preserves."

"She wore a joyous smile and a giant pink hat with feathers to church. Had a baggie full of hard candies in her purse and was always pleased to offer you some."

"And she died at the ripe old age of ninety-four."

"Died in her sleep, dreaming of Elvis."

"Skinny Elvis, before the movies," Genie said.

Calvin nodded.

"Sleep well, old Lily." Genie's voice was rawhide.

The two offered a moment of silence, then headed back to the shed with the tools. Calvin didn't think either one of them believed their own lie. Six feet under the dirt they'd leveled was a young girl who, up until recently, still dreamed of having her own pony and wore an Easter dress with a ribbon in her hair, one that probably matched the same ribbon on the wreath.

CHAPTER 23

CALVIN WAS RIFLING through one of the drawers in the kitchen when he found the map, rolled like some biblical scroll hidden amongst errant rubber bands and pens that no longer wrote. He unfurled it on the countertop and looked at the image. It was the cemetery, blocked off in grids and small rectangles. There were names neatly printed on the ones occupied, beneath each name a numerical date. Month and year.

Genie came out from the back bedroom and stopped by his friend. "Whatchya got there?"

"Map of the graveyard. Names and dates for the plots in use. Names in red for the ones paid for but still empty." He reached into the drawer again and came out with a handful of loose tacks. Calvin tacked the map to the wall above a Formica table covered in coffee stains.

"Not exactly fine art." Genie sat down at the table and resumed drinking his coffee, grown cold.

"Figured we could use it for reference, the lay of the land."

Genie nodded, then winced as he drained the last of the coffee. "Well, right now I'm gonna go refer to the john, then we'll see about edging the parking lot. And trim the hedges. Damn things grow like weeds."

Calvin nodded and stood still, studying the map.

While Genie was in the bathroom, Pastor Rosem knocked on the threshold of the open door. "Good afternoon, Calvin." The pastor wore his priestly garb, but his thinning hair was slicked back, rather than the combover the men were used to seeing. Calvin thought it made him look younger somehow.

"Afternoon, Pastor."

"Unfortunately, I've got some grave work for you boys. Lost one of our own. Just found out yesterday. Her parents are beside themselves. God bless 'em."

Calvin thought about the conversation he had with Genie earlier that day, about never wanting to know the age of those whose beds they were making. The universe didn't seem to give a shit about that wish.

"Sorry to hear that." Calvin pulled a chair out from the table for the pastor.

"I can't stay. Just wanted to give you the plot where you'll be digging. May as well get it done today. Burial's the day after tomorrow. Supposed to stay dry but put the tarp over it when you're done just to be safe." Pastor Rosem eyed the map, nodded toward it. "Good idea. Put a tack in plot 112. That's where Wendy will be buried. It's near a big oak, so you may have to wrestle with some roots. There's an ax in the shed, but Bunyan himself couldn't split a melon with it. So probably head down to the hardware store. Fred Willis owns it. I added your names to the church's tab. Just tell him I sent you. Any time you fellas need a new shovel, rope, or any tool, just put it on the tab and keep the receipt."

Genie made his exit from the bathroom, nodded at Rosem. "Pastor Rosem."

"Good afternoon, Genie. Was just telling Calvin here the Birdsongs lost their daughter."

Genie eyed Calvin as if acknowledging their desire to not hear the details, and yet here they were.

"Calvin's got the plot number, but you'll most likely have to cut through some roots. Quite the tree providing shade in that area."

"Now that we've got you here, I thought you should know we found a grave that'd been tampered with," Genie said. "Either that or your son liked to leave the holes half-finished."

The pastor's brow furrowed like he'd just smelled something he'd rather not have. "My son?"

"You said he used to have our job. Matter of fact, we met him a few days ago. Didn't seem too happy to see us," Calvin said.

"On the grounds or in town?"

"Right here on the grounds, belly full of spirits."

"And somethin' else," Genie added.

The pastor's eyes met the ground, and he was silent a moment. "You'd probably do best to stay clear of him. He's harmless, really. But he's not in a good way these days." He looked back to Calvin and Genie. "I take it you repaired the grave?"

"We did. He didn't desecrate it exactly, just didn't finish it, I'm thinkin'," Genie said, keeping the occupied coffin story to himself.

"Or was digging it up," Calvin added.

The pastor gave a quiet chuckle. "Jimmy didn't exactly take pride in his work, but I'm praying for him. We all are. He'll find his way. But until then, pay him no mind should you cross paths again. Seeing you fellas may set him off. I wouldn't say he misses his job, but I'd guess it makes him sour to see another with it."

"I can understand that," Genie said. "Every man needs a job. Without one, you don't feel . . . whole."

"He'll get by. God will see to it."

Calvin supposed God had done the same for him and Genie, letting them "get by." But those words had different definitions for different folks. For them, it was waking up with a smile on their faces despite their situation, as well as bellies full of food, even if that food was someone else's scraps.

"One more thing," the pastor said. "The graves here, we don't dig six feet down, and the coffins aren't vaulted. Crownover being a mining town, there's a whole maze of tunnels down below. No more than four feet is fine."

Calvin's eyebrows flew up like two startled caterpillars. "Four feet? That even legal?"

The pastor smiled—a thin line that felt passive-aggressive, meant only to stave a boiling pot inside. "It is here. The nearest cemetery is thirty miles away, and the locals like to stay local, So we make it work, just like New Orleans, where they bury their dead above ground."

Calvin shrugged and thought how that made their jobs easier, and if he was honest, digging for hours at a time was something he wondered if his back could even handle. "You're the boss," was all he said.

The pastor scanned the room, seeming to take note of the cleaning they'd done. "Lookin' good, fellas. Glad you're settled in, and I'm looking forward to seeing you in church on Sunday."

The words caused Calvin and Genie to trade glances. "We'll do our best," Calvin said. He wasn't sure if that was a lie or he meant it.

"Until then," Pastor Rosem said. "I'll be around." He walked out the door, stopped, and turned. "I think it'd be a nice gesture if you attended Wendy's funeral."

Genie stepped forward, concern across his face. "I'm not sure it would, pastor. We don't exactly have the attire for that. We've got two sets of clothes, and you're looking at the best of 'em."

The pastor waved a hand. "It's not the clothes that matter but the heart. You'll be fine." Then he walked away.

Calvin looked at his friend. "I doubt a couple strangers showing up at a girl's funeral wearing the clothes they slept in is gonna win points with the locals."

"Took everything I had not to roll my eyes . . . and by the way, thanks for locking us in for Sunday service."

"The hell was I supposed to say?"

"I don't know, but I know how I feel about church. What me and God have, that's between Him and me, not some room fulla oversized bonnets and stiff suits. A person doesn't need a special building or liaison. You either know Him or you don't."

"Let's just get through this funeral first, then you can bitch about hittin' the pews."

CHAPTER 24

THEY MET FRED WILLIS at the hardware store. Fred was older than them by at least five years, maybe ten. His thin legs swam in a pair of green Dickies, while his head sat under an old fishing hat sporting a button that said, "I Like Ike."

He showed the men around the store, and it seemed to Genie the old man was lonely, looking for any reason to strike up a conversation, keep them longer than need be.

As they walked, the wooden floor creaked, and each step was an audible welcoming. It made Genie feel the same way a winter fire's amber glow cast upon a living room did. Homey, comforting. He hadn't seen that glow in decades, but this sound was the next best thing—boots on worn wood, where countless men had walked, searching for tools to get a job done. Each creak a vault stocked with years. The smell of nails and fertilizer. It put a smile on his face.

Fred had a kind voice, full of passion for his job and for people in general, especially men looking for tools. He found them an ax, took note of the cost, and added it to Rosem's tab. "Digging near a tree, huh?" Fred said over the counter as he stuck a pencil behind his ear.

"Yessir," Genie said.

Calvin nodded, distracted by a young boy who'd walked in, reading the tiny comic wrapper from a piece of Bazooka gum.

Fred lowered his voice, leaned in. "I suppose you'll be digging Wendy Birdsong's grave. Maybe that's what the ax is for?"

Calvin pulled away from the boy and his gum wrapper. "We're just here to do whatever needs done, sir."

"Call me Fred."

"Okay, Fred. Appreciate you helping us find the ax. I'm sure we'll see you around."

"Anything you fellas need, anything at all, come on down. I even got some new drills in. Cordless. Sure, they're costly, but you'll get any job done in half the time."

"Thanks, Fred," Genie said. "We'll keep that in mind."

He threw out a few more words just before the two walked out the door. "Ten percent off, whatever you need. And what I don't have here, I'll happily order."

"Mighty kind, Fred." Genie nodded.

"Thank you," Calvin said.

The door opened, the bell above it rang, and the sun beamed down.

"Damn, that Fred's a good egg," Genie said.

"Met a few now, haven't we?"

"Stop and get some ice cream or head to work?"

"Thought we were holding onto the last few bucks. Besides, a six-foot-three black man holding an ax in the middle of a town where no one knows his name and the sheriff wants him gone. You tell me."

Genie's belly bounced through a chuckle that triggered a quiet cough. He shook his head but maintained the smile. "Work it is." Then the smile melted. "Speak of the devil."

Calvin followed Genie's eyes and saw Sheriff Mallon heading their way with quick steps and a determined stride.

"Shit," Calvin spit through gritted teeth and a plastic smile. He gave a friendly wave. "Sheriff Mallon. Beautiful day, isn't it?"

The sheriff shortened the distance between them and stopped, his chest puffed out, thumbs hooked in his belt. "What in the four-legged fuck are you still doin' here?"

"On our way to work." Genie nodded toward the ax in his hand. "Had to make a stop at Fred's."

"Fred's? What the . . . What do *you* know about Fred?"

"I know he's a helluva guy who likes to talk and offered us ten percent off everything in there." Calvin threw a thumb behind him, toward the hardware store.

"I know you think you're workin' for Pastor Rosem . . . " The sheriff's eyebrows did a little dance.

"We sure are. We're the new caretakers over at the cemetery." Genie tried not to smile.

"Not for long, you're not." The sheriff's aggressive tone caught the attention of a passerby, and he looked their way.

"Listen, Sheriff," Calvin said. "We're not here to start trouble. We came out west looking for work, and we found it. It's honest work, and we're honest folks. You'll get no trouble from—"

"I was lenient on you boys the other day. I won't do that again. If I see you in town tomorrow, you'll be shittin' in a bucket for at least the next week, until I figure out what to do with you."

"Guess you'll need to take that up with your deputy then, as well as the pastor," Genie spoke up. "Because they was the ones what made this happen."

Sheriff Mallon's eyes turned to slits, and his top lip curled into a smile that carried no joy. "The deputy, eh?"

"And the pastor of *your* church."

"Here's the thing about Deputy Wayne." The sheriff's eyes were drilled into Genie's. "He don't know coons like I do. He's a baby with a badge. Don't know shit about life or what kinda downfall comes to a town where you let monkeys run free."

Genie's chest tightened, and he felt a cough coming, but he held it.

For all of two seconds.

The air rushed out of his lungs like he'd been squeezed by God, and the cough rushed forward. Specks of blood spattered the sheriff's face, and he winced, hand to his holster in a swift, knee-jerk movement. The sheriff threw his other arm up and covered his face, then wiped it and saw the blood.

"You dirty fuckin' nigger."

"Whoa, Sheriff." Calvin threw himself between Genie and the cop. "Law or not, you watch your mouth."

"Sheriff!" The call came from the park across the street. Calvin turned to see Deputy Wayne jogging toward them, hand on his baton to stop it from banging into his leg.

Mallon side-eyed the younger cop, a sneer on his face. "Whatever it is can wait, Deputy. I'm dealing with these two. That one just spit blood on me. Filthy black fucker." Mallon slid his gun free as he spoke, and they all saw his hand shaking.

Wayne hustled over and stepped between the sheriff and the two men. He whispered to the sheriff, but it was more of a hiss. "There are people watching, and dammit, Sheriff, it ain't 1960. We're all kin here. Now, slide that gun home, and I'll send these men back to work. You don't . . . " Then the deputy's voice went quiet as a mouse fart. "And we both know what happens."

"You threatenin' me, boy? I'll slap you so hard you'll be shittin' out next week's dinner. Now, get outta my way." Mallon turned the gun around so the business end was clenched in his fist handle-like. With his other arm, he pushed Wayne aside to deal with Genie. The sheriff's face burned red when he saw the old men were gone. He squinted to make out their shrinking forms as they hoofed it down the street.

He turned to Deputy Wayne. "You're in it deep now, puddin'. Real fucking deep. You holdin' your bullshit over my head. That ends now. Do what you gotta do, but I'll be damned if I'll let some shit-smear like them stink up *my* town." Mallon said the words like they were snot in his throat, practically spat them.

"You sure about that?" Deputy Wayne hadn't backed down. There was no hint of being intimidated by his superior. Whatever war they had going on, both men stood strong against the other, with no sign of give.

"Go home for the rest of the day, Deputy."

Mallon stomped down the street to his office and slammed the door closed behind him. The few gawkers in the street went back to their business.

Wayne stood in the hot sun, feeling as cold as the bottom of a lake.

CHAPTER 25

THE SUN WAS slinking behind the clouds on its way to the horizon. The shadow of the moon trailing, though night was a few hours off.

"Your heart slow down yet?" Genie looked at Calvin as he hunched, hands on knees, a long string of saliva connecting his bottom lip to the ground. The smaller man just shook his head.

"Mine neither. You believe that shit?"

Genie chuckled, but it was hollow. Making light of something awful had always been their balm. Their way to deal and cope. This felt different. This wasn't a shopkeep yelling them off for appearance's sake or some kids trying on bravado. This was a cop. A man sworn to protect but who damn near seemed like he was about to kill a black man in the middle of the street in broad daylight.

"Put it out of your head, big man. We got a job to do, and that poor girl just needs a bed. Don't need us jawin' about injustice. A young girl dying is injustice enough." Calvin stood and wiped his face on his forearm. He looked at his friend, saw the dark stains on his chin and the neck of his shirt. Something sharp slid into Calvin's heart and turned. He smiled at Genie but didn't say a word. If Genie wanted to talk about it, he would. "I'm gonna grab the wheelbarrow and the tools. You rest a bit more."

Genie nodded but grabbed the one shovel that was leaned against the shed and headed toward plot 112. Once there, he put his heel to shovel and bit dirt with it, heaving it gently behind him and to the side. By the time Calvin showed, the topsoil was gone with careful cut edges where they'd already measured and staked the grave using twine.

"Care to get your hands dirty while I sit a spell? Don't wanna hog all the fun."

"Mighty generous of you," Calvin joked.

Genie let all of five minutes fly before grabbing the shovel again and joining in. They dug until the tentacle-like roots stopped production, then Genie swung the ax, severing a thick tangle of roots from the ancient tree. Within a few hours, the hole was dug, and the last sliver of sunlight cast long shadows across it. Four feet deep. They stared down at the shallow grave, where a girl named Wendy would sleep forever.

"Don't seem like much, does it?" Calvin mumbled as they stood near what he assumed was the head of the grave, rubbing at the palms of his aching hands.

"It's enough. Got to be. From dirt we came and back we go. Breathed into life and that breath drawn back. Got to be enough." Genie spoke clear, and his voice was deep with conviction.

CHAPTER 26

THE NEXT DAY went by in a blur. They kept to the undertaker's cottage and the cemetery grounds. No sign of the deputy or the sheriff, though they expected at least one to show at some point, either the deputy to reassure them everything was fine, or the sheriff to assure them everything was not.

Pastor Rosem blessed them with a brief visit, just long enough to deliver a plate of leftover roast beef and praise them on a job well done regarding Wendy's grave. He also threw them a reminder about attending the burial and then church on Sunday. Neither man was excited about either event.

The day of the burial, Genie looked at the coffee pot on the stove, at the little clear glass bulb on top, waiting for it to burp when the liquid began to percolate. The clock was slowly moving to eight. The burial set for ten. Then he and Calvin would stand awkwardly by, itchy inside, waiting for the mourners to leave so they could finish their job, the shoveled dirt hidden under a tarp like some dirty secret that whispered, *Yes, once you leave, the girl gets covered forever.*

Genie could hear Calvin's dragging steps in the hall, followed by the closing of the bathroom door. He turned off the burner, pouring the two mugs full of steaming black coffee, then carried them to the table and sat down, sliding Calvin's mug to the other side of the small table. His antsy eyes stole another look at the clock. It was almost a quarter after.

"So much for that watched pot nonsense," he muttered.

"Talkin' to yourself now?" Calvin slid into his chair and gripped the warm ceramic of his cup.

"Mighta been."

Calvin noted the deep circles beneath Genie's eyes and the weariness that settled on him like a shawl.

"You didn't sleep at all, did you?"

"A little."

"Liar. I heard you in there. Whispering. Pacing. Genie, it's all right. We just pay respects and stand quietly in the back, then tuck her in after everyone goes. It's our job."

"I can't help but think of that little girl on the train. I was tempted to tell Louise when I was writing to her last night but . . . "

"Don't tell a soul. Not a one. That's our burden to shoulder. If things were different, and this place was warm enough to call home, and the main lawman didn't have it out for us, we could sound the alarms. But a dead girl on a train we were on? Hell no. We mention a word of it, and we're as good as guilty. You know that."

"I know." Genie emptied his cup and sat it down. He looked at his friend, seemingly much smaller on his side of the table. Smiled at him with sad eyes, leaned back in his chair, and cracked his back. "But if this is the way it's gonna be, standing between Mom and Dad while they fight, I don't want that. There's other towns."

Calvin sipped the hot liquid and gave a breathy sigh. "I hear you. We deserve better."

"So, what's keepin' us here? Pride?"

"You forget about that cloud you're sleepin' on in there, old man?" Calvin threw his thumb toward the hallway.

Genie nodded and offered a sliver of smile.

"Not to mention free meals at the church. And we ain't even hit the potluck yet. Or Sunday donuts."

CHAPTER 27

GENIE STOOD UNDER a pine tree, his big body leaning on its trunk like a child finding comfort in a mother's leg, scared of the nearly one hundred strangers congregating not twenty feet from him.

Calvin rubbed a coin in his pocket, eyes on the ground. The night before, both men had scrubbed the knees of their pants the best they could, trying to get rid of the dirt stains. Genie nearly ripped a hole in his so stopped and figured a little dirt was better than a fringed hole.

The funeral brought folks of all ages, though Genie couldn't help but notice every one of them was white. So far, no stink eye.

A man with a stony face, who Genie assumed was Wendy's father, held tight to a woman who spent most of the time with a tissue balled up under her nose. Her face looked like it was melting, not from the running makeup around her eyes as much as the corners of her mouth and how they succumbed to gravity, like a fish's mouth. When she gulped for air between cries, it only added to the image.

When the pastor parted the crowd, stepping to the front where he could address them all, Genie could see a large posterboard full of photographs. Some of the pictures were of a baby, then a toddler. But most were of a young teenage girl with a smile full of teeth lined with braces. Wendy Birdsong.

Calvin kept his head down, whether it was out of grief or just paying respects, Genie wasn't sure, but he thought he should join him. Staring at people experiencing their worst felt wrong, voyeuristically so.

Before he lowered his head, he took one last glance at the posterboard, getting an image of her in his mind's eye for proper grieving meditation, when the largest picture, what looked to be probably the most recent, caught his attention more than he'd have liked.

He squinted, zeroing in on the girl's eyes, her hair, the shape of her chin. He stepped forward, unaware of his own movement. Behind him, Calvin whispered, but Genie couldn't hear him. He was hypnotized with fright, that what he was in the middle of discovering might be true, but please God don't let it be.

By the time he'd found himself within the crowd, his speculation turned to absolute truth, and the revelation filled his gut with molten lava. He turned and briskly walked back to Calvin and back to the mother's leg.

"Aww shit, Cal. Dammit, fuck, and hell too." It was meant to be whispered quieter than it was. A few heads turned.

"Calm down, we'll leave. We made our appearance."

"It ain't that." Genie's brow looked as though two invisible thumbs were pushing the skin together, and his eyes held the kind of worry Calvin hadn't seen on any man's face since the war. "That girl . . . Wendy. She's the one from the train, Cal. She's the dead girl from the train."

CHAPTER 28

THE SUN WAS just setting when they called it a day. They were exhausted. The two men had retreated to the shed and calmed each other enough to finish their duty once the crowd had dissipated. They'd checked in on Jimmy's bed. He wasn't there, and it was impossible to tell if he had been.

It took them less than an hour to cover the grave and smooth it flat as they could, laying the sod they'd sectioned off back over. When they were done, the finished job looked as though they'd done this type of work their whole lives. The only hard giveaway to the fact there was a grave there at all was the wooden stake at the head of it with the number 112 written in grease pencil, acting as a marker for the plot and a placeholder for the headstone.

They sat at their small table, staring at the cups of long-cold coffee. Not really seeing the dark liquid but gazing through it, into that place where minds went when trying to flee. Every few minutes, one of them would shake his head slightly.

The knock on their door would have startled them had they been paying attention. It was the third cluster of knocks on the door that brought them from their somber meditation and caused Calvin to rise from his chair.

"Pastor." He greeted their visitor and stepped back, allowing the man entry.

"Calvin. Eugene." He smiled, but it was bent slightly. "I just wanted to make sure you fellas were okay. You departed rather hastily from the service, and if I may say, Genie, you were white as your friend here. Ain't sick, are you?"

"No." Genie's voice was a hinge longing for oil. He let the terse reply hang a bit before he continued. "No, Pastor, just been so long since I was at a funeral, it brought back some unpleasantry."

"All to do with a funeral is unpleasant, friend. But I get it."

Rosem looked to Calvin, who was fretting with a thread on his shirt tail. The man put his hand on Genie's shoulder and spoke softly. "You get some rest. Tomorrow is a fresh canvas of a day."

Genie nodded and smiled up at the preacher. "Thanks. I'll be okay. Just . . . caught off guard."

"I don't suppose you've seen my son around again, have you?"

"No, sir. We haven't."

"Hmm . . . Must be back at school after a brief visit."

"Must be."

"Before I forget, I was going to see if you fellas wanted to come over for supper this evening. I'm making a pork butt in the Crock-Pot. If you can't make it, I'll bring by some leftovers tomorrow sometime." He patted the bigger man's shoulder and turned to leave. "Take care of one another, fellas. And thanks again for doing such a fine job for Wendy."

The screen door swung closed with a muted bang. Calvin slid back into his chair, and they waited for the sound of Rosem's footfalls to fade.

Genie spoke. "I don't like how easy the lies come these days."

"Considering the position we're in, I don't see that as a bad thing."

"You know me, Cal. I ain't no liar."

"I know you're not. Now, let's map this out. Weigh it some. Pros and cons. We know who killed that girl, least we know the faces."

"And at least one of their names," Genie said.

"But . . . we killed 'em."

Genie swallowed a stone that weighed more than he could handle. The words Calvin said he never thought he'd hear aloud. They were the same words he repeated those first few nights while trying to find sleep but somehow fought them off the next few. And now they were given more life than ever, tattooed on his brain and there to stay. Another part of him wondered why he gave a shit about those boys at all, especially after seeing pictures of the girl they'd raped, once so full of life, now in a box waiting for the worms.

"The one fell, right? That was his doing. Karma pulled him under," Genie said, but he wasn't so sure he believed it. A statement like that didn't seem to fit guilt's agenda.

"You're right, Genie. Guess I'm the only one who killed anyone, kicking the other boy out like that."

"Self-defense, Cal. You was helping me. I was a dead man, remember?"

"Except he'd stopped fightin' you before then." Calvin seemed to take a moment to replay the scene. "Either way, how it's laid out is if we go to the sheriff and—"

"Ain't goin' to the sheriff. No how," Genie interrupted. "Deputy Wayne."

"Okay, if we go to Deputy Wayne, tell him we were on a train with a dead girl, they find those two kids, it don't look good, especially when word gets to the sheriff. And it will. Has to. When he hears it, he'll put it all together, even if it doesn't make sense. He'll paint a picture of two lonely fellas—one being a colored— strangers in town, girl was raped on the same train they rode, then when they find the boys, that's just two more pieces in a puzzle he'll make damn sure fit together."

They sat quietly, a doom-filled cloud hanging over them. A tear dropped from Genie's eye and hit the table, then he coughed himself into a fit that lasted longer than most. Calvin watched him closely, struggling not to shed his own tears.

CHAPTER 29

GENIE LAY IN BED, staring at the moonbeam that lit the far wall. Just a rectangle the size and shape of a tiny door. He found his lips raising in a smile as he thought about how wonderful it would be if it opened and let him escape into a magical place like in a storybook.

After ten minutes of waiting for his eyes to tire, he grabbed his pen and paper and wrote a letter to Louise, telling her everything, spilling it all. For a short while, it felt good to get it off his chest, but then it didn't. He stood and went out to the main room, to the door, opened it and stared through the screen. The gravestones were painted lunar white, grass glistening from a light sprinkle that'd come and gone. Shadows shifted as a breeze brushed the trees and brought the smell of freshly cut grass. Something moved above him, in the trees, and he thought about the nonsense Jimmy Rosem spouted and looked up with a little apprehension.

"You can't sleep standing up, old man," Calvin said from his room down the short hall.

"Can't sleep anyhow."

"You doing all right?" Calvin got out of bed, walked down the hall and into the main room, where Genie's eyes bulged with tears and bags hung under them like two moonlit leeches.

"I can't hold it in, Cal. It ain't something I want to take to the grave."

Calvin put a hand on his friend's shoulder. "The grave ain't no time soon, my friend."

Genie nearly told him right then about the piece of paper in his pocket that said otherwise, that the grave was right around the corner. But everything else was burden enough. He would go this one alone. Calvin had been good to him, always been there. The stories they could tell. They were brothers indeed.

"If it makes you feel better, we'll head down to see Deputy Wayne in the morning, have a sit down, tell him what we know about the girl and about the boys and what they did. But you think me pushing the one out can be a secret you can keep?"

Genie turned from the screen door and looked at Calvin. "That one I can fit in the casket with me, brother."

CHAPTER 30

THE TWO TOOK their time with their morning coffee, sipping on the cups like they were savoring the last beverage they'd ever have. An hour from now, they could be behind bars, so there was no real desire to rush through the last bit of freedom.

"You know, there's a damn good chance the evidence they got from that girl was enough to link up to them boys. A damn good chance," Calvin said.

"You mean like fingerprints?" Genie sipped his coffee that'd started growing cold.

"Fingerprints, and whatever else they got up their sleeves these days. This is 1979, not 1800s Whitechapel."

"Then let's pray on that."

"Been prayin' all night, my friend." Calvin tipped the rest of his cold coffee and set the empty cup down. The sound rang out like an alarm that said it's time to go.

Genie gulped his, and the two went through the door, murmuring prayers that'd seemed to have gone stale.

***

When they walked into the police station, Genie let out a sigh of great relief after seeing no sign of the sheriff. The deputy sat at a desk on the far side of the room. A secretary, with enough hairspray to act as kindling with even the thought of flame, sat at a bigger desk that covered her from the neck down.

Deputy Wayne was on the phone, a smile on his face. He seemed to be in good spirits. He needed to be, Genie thought.

The secretary asked if she could help them with something, and Calvin did the talking.

"We're here to see Deputy Wayne."

The secretary swung her head around, looked at the deputy.

"He's on the phone right now, but if you can wait, I'm sure he'll only be a minute."

"Thank you, Ma'am," Genie said through a voice that cracked like his balls had just dropped.

The two scanned the room. Another pair of desks, a couple of doors that led to other rooms, and a hallway that grew dark as it rounded a corner. Before that corner was the holding cell they'd spent some early-morning hours in not too long ago. Genie hoped he'd never see that cell again.

"Hey, fellas." Deputy Wayne stood from his desk and waved them over, then pulled two chairs from another desk and put them next to his. "Have a seat."

Genie's feet felt shackled already. His heels scuffed the cement floor, like they were trying to stop him from doing what his conscience demanded.

"Hey, Dottie," the deputy said to the secretary. "That was Tim. He's headed over real quick for a couple dollars. Can you give him a few from the drawer and I'll replace it later?"

"You spoil that kid, ya know," Dottie said back.

"A boy like that, you would too."

"Sorry, fellas. Well, I'm glad to see Sheriff Mallon didn't scare you off. I told you I'd handle him."

"We appreciate that, Sir," Genie said.

The deputy chuckled. "Sir? We're long past that, aren't we?"

"Sorry . . . Deputy Wayne."

"Better. Now, to what do I owe the pleasure of this visit? After the events from the other day, I'd have thought I'd never get you in town again."

"Well . . . " Calvin began, knowing that Genie would need to be unwound and led like a timid dog on a leash. He stopped speaking and looked over at the secretary, Dottie, and back at Wayne. "Could we talk in private?"

Wayne's smile diminished slightly, and he nodded. "Hey, Dottie. You mind going down to the stand and grabbing brunch? A burger for me. Fries. And whatever you want. Fellas?"

"Thank you, we just ate." They hadn't. Neither of them could stomach the idea of a meal.

"Just us then." He fished out his wallet and pulled free a ten, then hustled to Dottie's desk and set it down.

Dottie rose and smoothed her blouse, grabbed the money. "I'll be back in about fifteen then." She nodded at the men as she walked out the door.

"Now. What's up, fellas?"

Calvin nodded and began to speak. "Deputy, you know Genie and me rolled into town just last week, and we slept in that old shack-house and Mallon brung us in . . . You know all that."

"Yeah." The deputy folded his arms, listened intently.

"And you know we headed out from Chicago, to try and make some honest living in our gray years."

"Right." The deputy's eyes trailed over their shoulders toward the door. "Hold that thought, Calvin. Tim's here, and now Dottie isn't. I gotta grab him that money."

"No worries."

Deputy Wayne stood up, a smile plastered on his face, and left his desk while Calvin and Genie pow-wowed.

"It ain't too late, Genie. You sure about this?" Calvin looked at his friend.

Genie nodded. "I'm sure. I been thinkin', and I got a good feelin' things'll work themselves out. Let's just pull this bandage off quick like."

Both men stared at the desk in front of them, the paperwork, nameplate, and stapler, a shoddy pencil holder that looked as though it'd been made by a grade-school kid in art class, misshapen clay smothered in too-shiny glaze. They listened while the deputy greeted the boy named Tim and gave him the money, then: "Hey, fellas. Want you to meet my nephew. My pride and joy, this kid." Both men turned in their chairs. "Tim, this is Eugene and Calvin. They're new to Crownover."

Calvin hid his shock better than Genie when they saw the boy's face. It was "Tony." The boy who raped and killed the girl they'd just buried.

The boy Calvin pushed from the train.

CHAPTER 31

"**Y**OU ALL RIGHT, Eugene?" the deputy asked.

Tim's own look of surprise dissolved quickly, morphing into a smirk that Genie took as, *I got you now, motherfucker.*

"Spittin' image of my great-grandson is all," Calvin said, trying for the recovery of an otherwise very awkward conversation.

Genie couldn't speak. Those sleepless nights, where he thought about this boy lying along the tracks, broken-boned and bleeding out until the maggots nipped at his eyes. Feeling sadness at youth lost unnecessarily, then remembering the deed that led to it, the anger swirling inside amongst the fear and sadness.

"Uncanny. Ain't it, Genie?" Calvin elbowed his friend hard, who finally closed his loose jaw.

"Uhh . . . yeah. For a second there, I thought it *was* him." Genie couldn't look away and anxiously awaited the boy's own response to the dark revelation.

"Welcome to Crownover, Mr. Eugene. Mr. Calvin." The boy nodded toward each of them. "Just passing through?" It was an invitation to get out of Dodge, an offer that'd become familiar.

"They're working over at Kimball Pines for Pastor Rosem, staying at the old parsonage house," Deputy Wayne said.

"I'm sure I'll be seeing you around then." Tim's smirking face was replaced by a mask, the same one he always wore around his uncle, who seemed to think the kid was a gift from God.

"No doubt about it." The deputy patted his nephew on the back. "In the fall, Tim helps rake leaves over at Kimball. This'll be your last year for that, though, won't it, Tim? Tell them where you're going next spring."

Genie wanted to smack the prideful smile off the deputy's face and tell him to wake the hell up, his nephew's a piece of shit that don't belong on the devil's shoe.

"UCLA," the boy said.

"Los Angeles, California." The deputy beamed when he said it. If it was night, the sparkle in his eyes just may have lit up the town. "He'll be rubbin' elbows with movie stars. Hell, maybe even decide to act himself and get famous!"

Genie coughed into his hand, and for a moment he thought he might vomit. He pulled away a wet hand and wiped it on the side of his leg. "Congratulations."

"Acting . . . I'll bet yer good at that, huh?" Calvin said through a smile made of lead. "Well, don't let nothing derail that bright future of yours." It was Calvin's own message, that as far as he was concerned, the kid's not safe. Somehow this'd get out.

"Oh, I won't. There ain't a thing in this world that'll stop me. Isn't that right, Uncle Jeremy?"

"You'd better believe it." Another pat on the back. "Listen, I hate to shoo you away so soon, but we were just knee-deep in something important."

"No problem. We can catch up tonight. Maybe after supper, we'll toss the ball."

"You got it."

"Nice meeting you." Tim gave a little wave of his hand, along with that smirk again, and as he turned to leave, Genie took note of his prized knife strapped to the boy's hip, nestled in a new leather sheath.

Genie and Calvin said nothing back. The charade had run dry.

The deputy found his seat back behind the desk. "Tell you what. I lucked out with that kid. He lost his dad in a fire, his mom just a couple weeks before that to cancer. Been raising him for the past six years. He's like my own."

Genie searched his mind for his next few words and which direction to take. There was no coming clean now. They'd have better luck with the sheriff, and that was no option either. Before Calvin took another route, Genie spoke up. "Deputy, we was just wanting to tell you about a vandal out at the cemetery is all. Someone . . . uhh . . . ripped a wreath apart and left some broken glass near one of the headstones. We thought we should report it."

"Yeah . . . and they tore up the grass, too," Calvin added.

"Vandalism in a graveyard. Doesn't get much lower, does it?" The deputy took his hat off and brushed his hair back, then topped it again. And that's when Genie realized it was an old deputy's hat he'd seen Tim wearing that night, not a ranger's hat. The image of the boy wearing it bubbled in his mind and made something squirm in his belly.

"No, it doesn't. But we'll try and keep a closer eye on things. I think it might have happened before we came along," Calvin said.

"Only so much you fellas can do. Ya can't sleep with one eye open."

"Suppose you're right. Though that ain't a bad idea." Calvin nodded to Genie, who said nothing for fear of his fake smile falling to the floor in pieces.

"Thanks, Deputy." Calvin stood and extended a hand to show they were through here.

"You sure that's all you needed? Seemed you were in duress, beating around the bush."

Genie stood, his knees popping like burning wood. "We just take our jobs seriously, Sir . . . uhh . . . Deputy Wayne. And we felt awkward having to come to you about anything so soon. That's all."

"As do I. Very seriously." The deputy offered a firm shake. "If it happens again, let me know. Hell, maybe I can even sic Tim on the case, find a few things out at school. He'd get a real kick out of that."

Yeah, I'll bet he would, Genie thought.

CHAPTER 32

HE TWO MEN stopped at the corner and watched the town's sole traffic light swing in the breeze. The cool kiss from the same slight wind caressed their foreheads and felt like the fingers of angels. Calvin's eyes were sunken back in small, wrinkled caves. Genie wasn't the only one who hadn't been sleeping as of late.

Calvin spoke first. "That little bastard knew exactly who the hell we were. And he knew we wouldn't say a word."

"Well . . . the good news is he's alive. The bad news is . . . he's alive. And the little shit has my knife." Genie looked in both directions before stepping from the curb. They crossed within the white lines of the crosswalk. Didn't need Mallon dragging them in for jaywalking. Would be a capital offense for sure.

Calvin turned to his friend. "So, we got a game plan?" He paused and tipped an imaginary hat to a young woman exiting the store they stood by. She smiled and walked briskly in the direction of the bank.

"Ain't much we can do. We either stay put and pay attention, until we think of something better, or we hightail it outta here. But . . . we do that, and I bet that little shit will sound the alarm that we was the ones what killed the poor girl, somehow he'd pull it off without getting himself tarred . . . and then we're done."

Calvin shook his head and leaned closer. "Nope. Fuck that. I'm too old for runnin' and too pretty for jail."

They stared into one another's faces, tanned from outside work and seasoned by time and circumstance. Genie chuckled out of disbelief that this had somehow gotten worse. The quiet laugh was an awkward thing. It stumbled and fell to the ground like it never happened.

Calvin pinched the bridge of his nose. "I can't think right now. I'm so caught off by that shit stain. His uncle doesn't know that boy

94

at all. He's raising Satan's spawn and can't even smell the brimstone. We gotta keep our heads about us. Pass off like nothing happened until we got a plan."

Just as they neared the front of the hardware store, a blue Dodge tooted its horn and swung in close to the curb, pulling barely past the portion painted yellow. Dottie rolled down the passenger side window and leaned over close to it.

"You fellas leaving? I got you each a cup of fries."

Calvin nodded and smiled. It was Band-Aid tight and uncomfortable. "Thank you, Ma'am, but we gotta get back to work. Appreciate the kindness, though."

"Nonsense. Here." The woman rummaged through a paper sack on the seat—grease stains in birthmark patterns—until she found two paper cups filled with French fries. "Lunch on the run. And you're most welcome." She handed them each their cup.

"Thanks again," Genie spoke as Dottie skooched back to her spot behind the wheel and put the car into gear. The engine whined a little as it idled.

They watched her slowly pull into the street and crawl the half block to her spot in front of the station before they commenced walking. Calvin wiped greasy fingers on his pant leg and chewed as he did it. He side-eyed Genie, watched him staring straight ahead, cup of fries clutched to his chest like a crown of gold.

"If that boy did kill that girl, he'll go to any length not to get caught. And I'm thinkin' his uncle might too, should he find out the truth. Two homeless men new in town with no family. Shiiit. Next grave we dig just might be our own," Genie said.

"We'll figure it out, Brother. We've got to." Calvin said the words but didn't necessarily believe them.

"I don't see how you can eat at a time like this." Genie didn't look at him when he spoke.

"Ain't wasting good fries. In fact, if you ain't gonna eat yours . . ."

Genie held his cup out, and the men resumed their stroll down the main street, toward the end of town where the cemetery was. Their hearts and minds were stuffed with eels of anxiety that swirled and bit.

CHAPTER 33

GENIE SAT ON his bed, pen in hand and halfway through a letter to Louise. He'd told Calvin he needed some time alone.

In the letter, Genie shared all about the deputy's son, telling her if given a chance to look through the kid's hair, he'd surely find a succession of sixes, just like in that movie that came out a few years ago. He wouldn't have otherwise gone to such a film, but the girl running the booth tossed them a few free tickets, a drink, and some popcorn. He didn't care much for the movie—half of which he slept through—but the popcorn was good, as was the comfort of the chair.

I can feel things changing, Louise. And not for the better. There are places in the world disguised as paradise but hold the same darkness the city does. It's like walking through a beautiful forest and tipping over an old log or a majestic rock and seeing the squirming bugs beneath. Keep us in your prayers when you speak to God. I think we'll need them.

Like most times after signing his name, Genie shed a few tears, triggering a coughing fit that ended in more blood. But this time it was pink, not deep red. He told himself things were getting better, as blood-tinged was better than pure crimson. Maybe the Colorado air was healing his old lungs.

Genie opened the small fridge and smiled, still not used to having a supply of food at his fingertips. He made a cheese sandwich thick with mayo and wished he'd saved his fries. He downed his lunch and headed outside.

Calvin was raking near the fence where leaves had trapped themselves against it. He wondered just how bad it got when fall came around.

"Missed one," Genie tried to joke, but Calvin didn't hear him.

So he wandered over to Wendy's grave. Now that he knew her killer was alive and doing well, offering some graveside words felt necessary. He hadn't even gotten to the grave when he noticed it was in the same sorry shape the other had been just days ago. Dirt thrown about, not flattened but slightly concave. He hustled over to Calvin.

"Cal . . . "

Calvin heard him this time and stopped raking.

"Wendy's grave . . . it's torn to hell like the other was."

Calvin stood with the rake in his hand, his face twisted into a look of puzzlement. "That means it wasn't Rosem's son half-assin' it. Someone's tampering with the plots."

Genie nodded. "But why? That don't seem like vandalism, just throwin' dirt around."

"You think someone's digging the whole grave right up?"

"Sounds crazy, I know. But that seems to be the world we live in these days."

Calvin itched behind his ear with the end of the rake handle. "Let's take a look."

The two walked over to the young girl's grave, stared at the mess. Calvin said, "I think you're right. This here's been dug up. How deep, who's to say?"

"Ain't that deep to begin with . . . Think it was Jimmy?"

"Could be. That boy's batshit crazy. But I'm wondering about Tim. If he'd seen us around town before today, makin' nice with his uncle, that's motive. Cuz he knows if we start squealing, they might dig her up like they do for investigations. But if there ain't no body there—"

"Then there ain't no evidence," Genie said.

"Exactly." Calvin shook his head, sighed. "I hate sayin' it, Genie, but I'm startin' to wish that boy had died when I pushed him off the train."

"What boy?" said a female voice.

The two looked up from the grave and saw a teenage girl coming out from behind one of the larger tombstones, a pad of paper in her arms.

Genie swallowed desert sand and wondered how hard the beds in prison were.

CHAPTER 34

"**YOU FELLAS GONNA** answer me?" She cradled the paper to her chest with one arm and used the other hand to tuck dirty blond hair behind her ear.

"You know it's impolite to eavesdrop, young lady." Calvin tried to look stern, leaning on the rake, steely eyes and all.

"Couldn't help it. I was sitting there minding my business when you fellas started talking all loud." She looked from Calvin to Genie and then back to Calvin. The two men looked at one another.

"What are you doing here anyway, hiding behind the stones?" It occurred to Genie maybe she'd been the grave meddler. Coincidence was like a stereotype: often kernels of ugly truth nested in it somewhere.

"Tracing tombstones," she replied as though it was the most normal hobby in the world, like collecting fall leaves to press in wax paper. "It's like spending time with the ones under."

"You're an old soul, ain't ya?"

"Who'd you push from the train?" Her eyes fixed on Calvin.

"Listen here. We was just talking about a story we heard on the news." Genie was ashamed of the lumpen lie as soon as it tumbled from his lips.

The girl smirked. "Bullshit. I was right over there, and I heard you. Someone dug up Wendy, and you think it was a boy you threw from a train, and now you wished he was dead." She smiled upon the recitation, proud as a kid in Sunday School who won the ribbon for memorizing her verse.

Calvin sighed heavily through his nose and stepped closer to Genie. "What now?"

Genie went toward the girl, who backed up a step herself. "Who are you, young lady?"

"Denise. Denise Wayne."

"As in Deputy Wayne?" Calvin asked.

"He's my dad. Not that he's aware of it these days. I'm just a shadow in the house. Shit . . . I spend more time at Dottie's house than I do at home. She's like the mom I never had."

Genie braced his forehead with an open palm, shook his head.

"Now, girl," Calvin said. "I find that unlikely. Deputy Wayne seems like a good guy from the—"

"Seems like it. But I'm the daughter he got instead of the son he wanted. If he hadn't lucked into inheriting my cousin, he'd be miserable."

Something sharp and icy pierced Genie's stomach, and he could tell from the look on Calvin's face he'd felt it too. The net of circumstance and coincidence was tangling around them. Soon they'd knot enough to keep them from being able to come up for air. They'd quite possibly drown.

"Tim?" Calvin asked. His voice was a dry husk.

"Ugh. Yeah. Him. He thinks he's fooled everyone, but not me. I know what kind of asshole he is." Her expression had retreated to a kind of distance, her eyes elsewhere while she mumbled.

"Why do you say that?" Genie asked, eager to see what this hive was going to issue from the poke.

"Why do you think he'd dig Wendy up?" she asked, ignoring Genie's question.

"Don't you worry about that none. We'll handle it."

The men watched the girl as she fidgeted her feet in the grass.

Calvin started raking the surrounding dirt onto the grave. "You gotta go, Denise. This isn't business to concern you."

"It might be."

Genie saw her eyes were threatening tears. Whatever was up with the girl, she was struggling and barely needed a twist to open her valves and let it loose. It hurt his heart to witness. She was a pretty thing, hair kept short, dressed like an old lady in a baggy sweater and loose jeans. He felt his lips tighten. There were flags here. Subtle things that sometimes belied abuse and trauma. He swatted that voice down in his head and said, "You don't need to tell us anything, girl. We're strangers."

"No . . . You're different somehow," she said and wiped an arm across her eyes. "If I can come in to use your bathroom, I'll tell you about the town a bit, maybe even why I don't like Tim. Unless you want me telling my dad you tried to kill a boy by pushing him from a train."

Calvin stopped raking, put a hand on his hip, then swept an arm toward the cottage. The three walked to the small house together, and the girl disappeared inside.

Genie looked at Calvin. "Skipping town just made the top of our to-do list."

CHAPTER 35

GENIE MADE THE girl a cheese sandwich and one with mustard for Calvin. He offered a mug of water for her and a cup of lukewarm coffee for him.

She talked through a mouthful of food, eating like she hadn't since the day before. "Where you guys from?"

Genie knew from here on out, pretty much everything he said would be a lie. He felt like God would understand under the circumstances. "New York City."

"You don't sound like New York people do in movies. What are you doing way out here?"

"We were looking for work."

"Why didn't you just look for work in New York?"

"The weather," Calvin said. "We got arthritis, does a number on our knees."

"Hmmm." She took another bite while the two stared at her, waiting for questions they didn't want to answer. "You drive here?"

"Took the bus after our limo broke down." Genie felt the tiny joke might help.

The girl ignored it and threw out the next question. "How do you know Pastor Rosem?"

"We met him when passing through. He needed help, we needed work, so here we are," Genie said.

Calvin folded his hands around his mug. "You sure are an inquisitive girl."

"Got to be." She stuck a finger in her mouth and worked a piece of bread from the roof of it. "This is my town. You guys are strangers with a strange story, and one of you tried to kill a kid." She smiled, fake as hell.

"Okay," Calvin said. "If you think we tried to kill a kid, why in God's name would you come in our house?"

"Because I think you're good people and the kid you tried to kill wasn't."

"We didn't try to kill nobody," Genie said. "We was on a train, and he fell."

"No . . . your friend here pushed him. I heard him say it. He said he wished the boy would have died when he pushed him. That's a direct quote."

Calvin grabbed his face and sighed.

"Ya know . . . " Another bite of sandwich. "When I was in your bathroom, I got to thinking. You said something about an uncle. You're talking about my cousin Tim, aren't you? He's the boy you pushed."

Genie had to sit down before he passed out. He grabbed a chair and deflated.

"Listen, girl . . . " Calvin said.

"Denise."

"Listen, Denise. What I said was kinda like a figure of speech. I didn't mean it."

"But you were talking about Tim, weren't you? What'd he do that you want him dead?"

Genie stared at the wall, wondering if they should just run now, grab the loaf of bread and cheese and haul ass.

Calvin looked at Genie. "She's not giving us much of a choice here."

Genie just shook his head in disappointment.

"Screw it . . . " Calvin looked back at the girl. "Tim tried killin' Genie on that train. He was trying to drag an old man to the door and push him out. So I pushed him. It was self-defense. That's that." It was mostly true.

"And what about Wendy and Andy? They hang out on those trains with him. They ride them all the time. And now Andy's missing and Wendy's dead."

"You think you're some kind of detective, huh?"

"Damn right. I can put the pieces together. I read Nancy Drew, Hardy Boys, Encyclopedia Brown . . . all that shit. I even watch *Columbo* sometimes."

Genie raised his eyebrows at Calvin.

"How old are you, Denise?"

"Almost fifteen."

The men just stared at her for a long minute.

"We have reason to believe your cousin and his friend killed Wendy."

Denise seemed to ponder the statement, then her tone changed, voice dropped. Her eyes went empty, like she wasn't there anymore but deep in thought, reflecting on something she'd rather not. "Did he . . . did he rape her?"

What she said made their spines twitch. Genie stood up from the table. "I can't do this, Cal. Get your stuff, and let's go." He started pacing the room, rubbing his forehead like he was trying to start a fire with it.

Calvin kneeled down level with the girl. "Why would you say that, Denise?"

The girl stared off, no focus in it. She said, "Because that's how he is."

"Cal . . . we got to move. We stick around here they'll make sure we got room and board for the rest of our lives, if you know what I'm sayin'."

Calvin put a hand up. "Just hold on, Genie. Denise . . . what do you mean?"

The girl finally broke her gaze and locked eyes with Calvin, swallowed hard. "You know what I mean." Small tears fled her eyes.

CHAPTER 36

CALVIN WANTED TO hug the girl and wished that boy was dead even more.

Genie stood, tapping his boot on the dirty floor, arms across his chest, eyes on the girl. "Listen . . . I'm sorry, Denise. It sounds like you got it real rough here, but—"

"I'm not gonna say anything about what you did," she said.

"There's nothing to say." Calvin spoke it soft and patted the girl on her shoulder, in a fatherly gesture, but she flinched back just the same.

She looked at him. "I think we know what you guys did and didn't do. You didn't kill Wendy. You did push Tim. But Tim is fine. No problem. So maybe you're right. There's nothing to say."

Calvin couldn't help but chuckle. "You're smart for your age, you know that?"

Since it was all on the table anyway, Genie let loose with a final confession. "Andy's dead. He's dead for sure. That kid went nuts. I mean he was losin' his mind on that train, Denise. I think he was high on somethin'. Trying to toss me into a tornado. We wrestled a bit, and I kicked at him. But I wasn't trying to get him off the train, just off me." His voice was shaky. "He hung on, and everything slowed down, like in a dream, like time stopped for just one unforgiving moment." His chin quivered, eyes glassy. "Then the wheels sucked him under." Genie stood by the window and looked out, wiped his face on a sleeve, pinched snot from his nose. "I kicked him off the train. It was him or me."

"They wanted you dead because of Wendy . . . " the girl said, her voice a gentle, forgiving breeze.

"That's how we see it," Calvin said.

"And now you think Tim dug her up to hide the evidence."

"It's lookin' that way, but we're not sure just yet," Calvin said, then knelt down again so he was at the girl's level, making sure she understood every word he was going to say. "Denise. Because you're so smart, and because I want you to trust us, I'm gonna be straight with you. Genie and I . . . " He was about to tell her they weren't from New York at all and they didn't ride a bus, and before last week they were homeless. But he felt it best they keep *some* secrets. Just in case. "We need this job pretty bad. It's more than money and a roof. Stakes are higher than that. And other than a few people, your cousin bein' one, we like this place quite a bit. There's a lot of good people here, like yourself. We've already noticed that."

"Lots of strange people here too," she said. "Wait'll you notice that."

"I think we've gotten a little taste of that too. But we're tired. We just want to be able to smile at the end of the day, close our eyes with a good conscience that we made a difference somehow, even if that difference is just working hard."

"Too deep, Cal," Genie said, making a gesture with his hand that what his friend just said went over the girl's head.

"What I'm trying to say is that we just want to mind our business, do our job, and eat our cheese sandwiches. So if you could keep all this between just us three, we'd appreciate it."

"Told you, I'm not saying a word. But only if you help me with something."

Calvin looked at Genie. "Sure . . . we can do that. Can't we, Genie?"

"Okay . . . let's hear it."

The girl darted her big eyes between both men and took a deep breath. "I want you to help me send my cousin to jail for what he did."

CHAPTER 37

BOTH MEN LOOKED at the floor, studying the scuff marks through the dust.

"Well?" the girl said.

"We're gonna need a minute, Denise," Calvin said. "There's more bread and cheese if you need another sandwich. We're gonna head outside and have a chat. Okay?"

"Do you have any cookies?"

"Sorry . . . no cookies. But there's some saltines in the cupboard, and a jar of peanut butter on the shelf above the sink, I believe." Calvin stepped toward the front door, and Genie followed, head weighted down like a cinder block rested on his neck.

The two walked outside, kept on for a good ten yards until they reached a tree. Genie put his big hand on it and leaned. "It's like we're cursed, Cal."

"Maybe we *should* leave, like you said. Wish the girl well, and when she makes for home, we high tail it."

"That was my kneejerk, for sure. But back there you was talking about laying our head down every night with a good conscience. We leave now, can we ever do that again? This girl's been through some hell, the kinda hell that's gonna stick like tar the rest of her life. And now she's asking for redemption, Cal. We ain't knights, and this ain't exactly shining armor, but we're all she's got. That idiot father of hers is blind as a bat, and she knows it. Lawman or not, she'll never tell her old man. But she told *us*."

"Dammit, Genie." Calvin kicked the tree and turned. "You're speaking too much sense right now, and the coward in me wants to pay no mind."

"You ain't the only coward, old friend. I had to spit them words before I wouldn't. And if I'm truthful, I regret spittin' them at all." He put a hand on Calvin's shoulder. "But we know what's right."

Calvin scanned the cemetery, the sky. He wiped his brow. "Aww hell . . . all right. But we gotta lay some ground rules. She can't be hanging around here. It won't look good. Especially if Mallon sees. He already has us painted as criminal trash."

"Agreed. And if Tim sees her anywhere near us, he'll suspect we told her or she told us and someone'll get hurt."

The two walked back to the cottage and went inside. Denise sat at the table, a package of open saltines in front of her, one of them in her mouth.

"Okay, Miss Marple," Genie said. "What's our first move?"

CHAPTER 38

DENISE SHOOK HER head and rolled her eyes. "You guys are acting like this is difficult. It's simple. You can't really go to my dad, so you go above him, to Sheriff Mallon. Tell him everything about what you saw on the train, about Wendy's grave, and about what I told you . . . you know . . . about Tim and stuff."

"No can do," Calvin said. "Mallon's got it out for us. He thinks we're trouble. *And* he's a racist. We tell him we were on that train, it'll make his day, cuz he'll pin every bit of it he can on us."

"Racist? Sheriff Mallon?"

"No doubt about it."

"Hmm . . . well, shit," Denise said, her head down, gazing at the coffee stains and cracker crumbs on the wooden table.

Neither man batted an eye at the kid's profanity. "He and your dad don't get along too well, do they?" Calvin asked.

"Not sure. I mean . . . I've never seen them get in a fistfight or anything, but they did have a falling-out once. I could never figure out what the deal was, but it had to do with my aunt."

"You talking about Tim's mom?" Genie said.

"Yeah."

"Cancer got her, no?" Genie hated that he'd said the word aloud, like it was a bad omen somehow, like he was giving life to his own ailment by acknowledging the power it held.

"Yeah. It was really sad. Everyone in town was a wreck over it, especially my dad and Sheriff Mallon. I'm thinking he lost someone like that before, and it maybe brought back some bad memories."

Calvin and Genie traded glances, putting the pieces together.

"Your aunt and uncle, they seem to have a pretty happy marriage?" Calvin asked.

"Not really. My uncle was an asshole. He didn't treat my aunt good at all. There were rumors he'd beat her. I remember seeing her bruised up a few times, but she always said it was because she's clumsy or had amnesia . . . something like that."

"Anemia," Calvin said.

"Yeah, anemia. She said it made her bruise easy, even just by tickling her."

"So then your uncle died in a fire soon after your aunt passed?"

"Yeah. He was drunk . . . fell asleep with a cigarette in his hand. It burned the whole house down."

"And that's when Tim came to live with you and your dad?"

"Yeah, he got custody. Then like a year later, he adopted him."

Genie chewed his lip before the next question. "And your mama?"

"She isn't around. Dottie Mayfield is the closest thing I've got. My mom left when I was just a baby. My dad said she stuck a note on my forehead that said, *'Thanks for the good time. Here's your door prize.'*" She smiled, but it was injured.

"Your dad told you that?" Genie fumed.

"Yeah. But for a long time, he said she was a model and worked in England and that she'd be back someday. Cops are good liars."

Genie went to touch the girl's hand, then thought better of it. "Sorry about all the questions, Denise. I know it ain't fun bringing this stuff up. But I think it might help with what we're dealing with."

She squinted her eyes, looked at Genie. "What might help? My ghost of a mother? My aunt and uncle?" She threw her eyes to Calvin. "How is that gonna help? They're dead."

"We're not sure yet, still putting the pieces together. But we may have enough to see the puzzle."

"I don't get it."

"When we find out more, we'll fill you in. But for now, there's not much to get. How about in a day or two we have another sit-down? Maybe we'll have more to work with by then."

Denise stood up and scooted the rickety chair under the table. "Okay. I'll be around." She turned to leave, then turned back. "Do you really think we can send Tim to jail . . . for everything?"

"We're sure gonna try," Calvin said.

Denise was quiet a moment, her eyes going glassy, looking at both men. "I'm glad you guys are here."

Genie felt his throat constrict and offered a tight-lipped smile. It'd been a long while since he'd heard such words directed at him.

CHAPTER 39

THE REST OF the day was spent making the rounds, checking off chores on their list of graveyard duties. They talked only briefly about what they'd learned from Denise and where to go from here. Mostly, they kept quiet, each of them brainstorming. They would have a full meeting that night at the cottage.

When suppertime rolled around, they headed to the church and grabbed dinner. Chili and hot dogs. Both of them poured the chili on their dogs and chowed them down with a heavy dose of onion. Calvin made a joke about their breath and how they'd killed any chance with the ladies. Gallows humor. Both men knew those days would probably never come again. Besides, Genie was sure even if they had, he'd run the other way. His heart still belonged to Louise.

Back at the cottage, they stayed up late, piecing things together during their meeting, coming to conclusions that felt like a lot more than speculation.

"You're gonna think I'm nuts," Calvin said. "But I think we need to speak with Jimmy again."

"You're right. I do think you're nuts. That man couldn't order a glass of sand at the beach, let alone fill in the blanks."

"We just got a load of useful info from a fourteen-year-old girl, Genie. She offered clues we weren't even lookin' for, and she didn't even know she was giving them. Jimmy's got a little brain left in there swimming in the acid."

Genie looked at the old alarm clock on the kitchen counter—12:30. "Guess now's a good time to see if Dracula's home."

***

With a flashlight in hand, they wasted no time getting to the shed. The graveyard at night was normally a peaceful place, with distant streetlights—and sometimes the moon—highlighting the stones, casting long shadows across the grass like fingers. But waking a crazy man from a coffin filled with the lingering reek of shit unsettled Genie.

They creaked the door open and directed the light onto the casket. Except where Genie's fingers had swiped it away, the thick layer of dust hid the black, glossy sheen of its lid.

"Should we knock?" Genie said.

Calvin rapped his knuckles on the lid. "Jimmy . . . you awake?"

"The fuck . . . !" A scream muffled by padded satin. "I am now."

Genie lifted the lid. The squinting man inside sat up on his elbows, shielded his eyes from the flashlight.

"Sorry." Calvin sent the beam toward the ceiling. "You got a few minutes?"

"We've got some questions," Genie said.

"This ain't my job anymore. Go ask my old man." Jimmy reached for the lid, and Genie held it tight.

"It's not about the job," Calvin said.

Jimmy's face changed, went slack. "You're talking about the kids."

Calvin and Genie locked eyes, then back to Jimmy. "What do you know about the kids?"

"You can hear 'em too?" Jimmy sat up straight, eager to hear their answer.

"Not sure what you mean, Jimmy."

"You can hear them, can't you? Screamin' from the church. I know all their names. I've got them memorized." Jimmy's eyes were wide, spooked and excited.

Genie looked at Calvin. "Told ya." He twirled his finger next to his ear, the universal sign for crazy.

"What kids?" Calvin's tone was a mixture of worry and impatience.

"Abby . . . Steven . . . Conner." He paused, counting the names on his fingers. "Bobby, Heatherlyn . . . Lily. Not Wendy yet, but that'll come. She'll be loud. Maybe as loud as Steven. If you haven't heard her yet, you will."

"These kids is talkin' to you?" Genie asked.

"No . . . just screaming. Hollering. Sometimes singing . . . You . . . you can't hear them?"

"No, we don't hear no kids screamin'."

"Jimmy . . . " Calvin said, ignoring the nonsensical talk and getting the conversation on track. "What do you know about Deputy Wayne and Sheriff Mallon?"

A look of confusion crossed the young man's face. "Wayne and Mallon? They've got nothing to do with this."

"We'll get back to the kids and their screaming, but tell us what you know about Wayne and Mallon's relationship."

Jimmy said nothing for a long moment that crawled slug-like as the two men waited. "Well . . . they can't stand each other."

"Any idea why that is?" Calvin said.

"Probably has something to do with the sheriff pokin' the deputy's sister."

"Yep . . . we put that one together. Didn't we, Cal?"

Calvin nodded. "Thanks to the clues Denise gave us."

"Not many know this. Hell, maybe just me and Wayne. But they were in love." Jimmy said the word *love* with an airy whisper. "I saw them twice out by the old shack, whispering sweet nothings, making love under the moon and all that. I think the deputy caught on and made them break it off before her old man found out."

"Love, huh? Sounds about right. Denise told us Mallon was shook up pretty bad over her death." Calvin steered back toward more questions, while Jimmy stared at the ceiling, watching spiderwebs in the rafters. Nodding his head as if to music that wasn't there.

"And then Tim's father died . . . what, a week or so later?" Genie said.

"Yep . . . whole house went up. Would have been gorgeous had there not been anybody inside." Jimmy lowered his voice, darted his eyes around the shed before continuing. "But you ask me, he deserved it. That man was a mean bastard."

"Worse than Mallon?"

"Mallon used to be different. After Kathryn died—"

"Kathryn . . . that's Tim's mother?"

"Yeah." With a quickness so fast it spooked both men, Jimmy threw his hands over his ears and shut his eyes. "Stop it! Just stop . . . I'm begging you, kids. I can't take the screaming."

The men waited for Jimmy to have what Genie hoped was a passing episode. Genie had had his own weak moments in that first year back from the war. He wasn't hearing voices, but when he closed his eyes, the same movies ran through his head—visceral and too much to bear.

Jimmy wiped his eyes, opened them. "After Kathryn died, Mallon changed. He's an asshole. But he ain't no drunk, and he doesn't beat his wife and kid . . . I mean, if he had one."

"Long as they ain't black, I suppose."

Jimmy's eyes squinted down to slits. "I don't get you."

"Mallon's a racist. Maybe you ain't seen it 'cause you're right in his eyes. But trust me, he don't like anything darker than a turkey leg."

Jimmy let out a chuckle. "You definitely don't know Sheriff Mallon. Why you asking about him, anyway?"

"I know enough to know he's an asshole, just like you said . . . "

"Mallon may be an asshole these days, but he's no racist. Kathryn . . . Tim's mom. Mallon's lover. She was black as night."

Genie's eyes lit the shed. "Hold on. Kathryn? Deputy Wayne's sister? White-as-the-moon Deputy Wayne?"

"She was adopted. But they didn't see it that way. She was always family, been a Wayne from day one. Barely had her cord cut."

CHAPTER 40

GENIE STARED AT the ceiling above his bed, catching his breath after a coughing spell. "So, we've got ourselves a theory on Wayne and Mallon, but Tim's momma being black puts a crack in it."

"The theory still has legs," Calvin said from the comfort of his own bed. "Though I can't help but wonder how much of what we get from Jimmy is nonsense. Like you said, he ain't right. When he shoved that beetle in his ear to stop the screams that weren't there . . . well . . . "

A quiet knock on the door.

Both men sprang out of bed, eyes locked on one another in the splintered moonlight. Genie clenched his fists—two meaty balls filled with aging bones. Calvin tiptoed down the hall and grabbed a butterknife from the counter, still covered in Jif.

Another knock, then a whispered, "Guys?"

A girl's voice?

Genie thought of the children's voices that plagued poor Jimmy. But this was real. Calvin had heard it, too.

The two crept toward the window and peeled back the curtain, just enough to see the fourteen-year-old girl standing on the weathered cement slab outside their front door.

"Dammit, girl," Calvin mumbled, his hand still gripping the dull knife.

Genie opened the door, wearing a disapproving frown. "A little late, no?"

"I snuck out." Her smile showed just about every tooth she owned.

"Aww hell, Denise. This can't happen. If we're gonna be a team, you've gotta play by the rules," Calvin said near the table, setting the knife down.

"He's right, little one," Genie said.

Denise let herself in and headed straight for the table, like it was the go-to for all future meetings, middle of the night or otherwise. She pulled a chair and sat down. "Who's Louise?" She was pointing toward a sheet of paper, the beginning of a letter Genie had started.

Genie snatched the paper away but didn't answer the question.

Tired of waiting, or already having lost interest, Denise said, "I wanted to tell you they found Andy."

Genie took a seat, dropped into it, let his arms swing by his side, his fingers nearly touching the dirty floor. He fixed his eyes on the distance, as far away as he could get.

"He was in a million pieces, all over the train tracks and in the grass," Denise said, a hint of excitement buried under the grim tone.

"How do you know that?" Calvin asked.

"Sheriff Mallon called Daddy at home, told him about it. I was listening on the other end. He didn't hear me though. I was real quiet."

"And then you snuck out and headed over here."

"Yep, thought you should know."

Genie shook his head and stood up. Paced the room. He turned to the girl. "We appreciate you telling us, but you here at night. It don't look good. If anyone sees you it'll make things a whole lot worse."

"Okay, I'll leave. Can I come over tomorrow?"

"Give us a few days," Calvin said. "We still have a job to tend to, which sounds like that'll include more grave digging, and we're still figuring out what to do about Tim and who to trust."

"Okay. I'll be by in a few days, but if you need me . . . " She grabbed a pencil from her back pocket and wrote seven digits right there in the wood of the old table. "That's my phone number. I almost always answer when it rings, but if my dad does, just hang up." Then she went to the front door.

"Girl . . . " Genie's voice boomed in the room, and her hand stopped on the doorknob. She turned to face them. "You be careful . . . mindful." Genie's tone was one of concern and warmth.

Denise smiled, then slipped out the door and into the night, leaving the men with grief in their hearts at the thought of another youth gone but with a strange kind of closure in the fact that at least the poor bastard had been found.

CHAPTER 41

THE LOOK ON Pastor Rosem's face was one of profound sadness and weariness. He looked tired and, for the first time since they had met him, his age.

Calvin stood in the doorway and stared for a little longer than was polite before he stepped back and let the man enter. Genie sat at the table nursing his coffee and holding the last of his toast. "Morning, Pastor."

Rosem just nodded and sat down across from Genie, in the chair that'd been Calvin's, until he was uprooted to answer the door.

"What's up, Preacher?" Calvin sounded irritable. They hadn't slept much, and he knew the reason for the visit. His coffee sat untouched and steaming a few inches from Rosem's hand. When Calvin leaned to grab it, he noticed the grime under the preacher's nails, and Rosem noticed him noticing.

"Couldn't sleep. Got up and did a little work in the flowerbeds. Culling what won't live the winter, covering what might."

A cocoon of silence was moving in, and the room grew awkward with it. Calvin sipped the coffee, then set the mug on the table in front of him.

"What's on your mind, Rosem?" Genie had had enough of the itchy quiet. "I can see you're bothered."

"I am, son, I am. I have lived in this town for nearly twenty-six years. I've seen people born and walked some home to their end. I have spoken for Jesus and made His promises to these people . . . " He glanced over at Calvin quick and then returned his attention to Genie. "And in the last few weeks, I've seen buried two of our children. That's why I'm here. Another child gone." The man paused while his chin quivered. "I'll spare you the details. It's just too heartbreaking." He rubbed at the corners of his eyes with a thumb and forefinger. "Death of the young ones . . . they get to me. They are to be the inheritors. The caretakers of the future. To see them snuffed . . . in such dark ways." The man's voice cracked, and his eyes leaked tears that streaked his cheeks. "These . . . These are the things that try my soul. My faith. And nip pieces from my heart."

The silence flexed again like a strongman's arm around them. Calvin pulled out the third chair and lowered himself into it. "Pastor, I know what you're saying, and I get how it must feel. Genie and I have seen ugliness. We've seen the face of death and counted his teeth. We've lived to speak of it. And if nothing else, that fear and that sense of hopelessness, somehow . . . some way, bolstered our faith in the design, the reason we're here and what for . . . " Calvin looked to Genie, who nodded and patted Rosem's forearm from across the table.

"Cal's right. You can break yourself down trying to understand the why and how of things. Good or bad. We get along by observing the here of 'em. We have questions, and we seek answers. We have prayers. We've asked for answers as much as anyone. We get them too . . . but sometimes. It's no. Sometimes . . . the answer we want isn't the answer we need." Though Genie believed every word he spoke, he couldn't help but feel like a hypocrite, seeing it was his boot that sent the kid to an early grave and the pastor here this morning.

"Thank you, fellas. But my struggle is for the children taken. They're too young to know their worth and their place in the scheme. They're plucked unripe. Put in the dark dirt when they ought to be dwelling in the house of the Lord forever . . . " He slipped back into a woolen silence, and the men just watched him. Minutes went by before the man stood up abruptly and stepped to the still-open door. "They're in my charge. Their eternity is around my neck, my yoke is their salvation." He smiled crookedly and nodded at the men. "Thanks for letting a tired and sad old man blather this morning. Sometimes my heart and head gets full and . . . "

"Ain't no need to apologize, Pastor. We're here for each other. That's how it's supposed to be anyway."

"You're good men. I'm truly grateful you're here, fellas. Thank you." A long, breathy sigh. "Funeral's in two days. Plot 274, right next to Andy's grandfather. Another good man." He shook his head and walked out into the cemetery, slowly made his way to the parsonage.

The fresh sunshine made the wet grass shine. The chill in the air was a reminder autumn was kicking in. Calvin and Genie watched the man disappear into the brick house and tried to make sense of the rambling they'd just heard.

CHAPTER 42

THEY HADN'T SEEN Denise in two days. The young girl was adhering to the rules. They did, however, catch a glimpse of the sheriff, once again glaring at them from his patrol car, scarfing down his lunch from Loretta's, while they worked the grounds. Digging Andy's grave was exceptionally difficult for Genie. He grew weak in mind and body through the chore, the cancer biting away at his insides, the guilt spreading like black ink through his mind, settling in the fissures. He held back tears through most of the task but broke down near the end. Calvin reassured him, using all the old tricks that normally worked, but this was different. This storm was the darkest of them all.

Calvin dangled his feet over the edge of the nearly finished grave. Genie sat with his back against a tree, wanting nothing to do with the hole. A middle-aged couple walked hand in hand along the stones, holding a bouquet of flowers. The two men watched as the couple set the flowers down on a distant grave and took a seat on the grass.

Genie caressed the scarf that hung loosely around his neck. "Who do you miss, Cal? Like really, truly miss?"

Calvin looked at Genie, saw him petting the scarf, and gave a tight-lipped smile. "My first wife, Sharon. Best cook that's ever put a plate in front of me."

"Oh yeah? You never talk about her."

"Probably 'cause I miss the hell out of her." He chuckled.

"Yeah, I get it."

"We were kids. I was just home from the war . . . didn't know shit about sacrifice . . . or communication. I knew about secrets though . . . and found out that keepin' them is never a good thing. They're seeds that never grow anything good. That last bit is on me, though. Hindsight taught me that."

Genie clapped the dirt from his hands, grabbed his shovel, and jumped in the hole to finish the job. "I know we're playing it cool for now. But I think we're forgetting something." He threw a shovel full of dirt over his shoulder and had to rest again.

"Go on . . . spit it out." Calvin moved his legs, stood up.

"Nailin' that boy ain't just for Wendy. She's dead. But Denise isn't. And if that little pecker is sneakin' in her room at night . . . "

Calvin shook his head. "Shit, bastard, and sonofabitch if that don't make us selfish, not givin' her grief another thought." He put the palm of his hands on the top of the shovel handle, rested them there. "So you're saying there's a chance his debauchery wasn't a one-time thing. That maybe this carries on still."

"We don't know that, and I ain't gonna ask the girl. But I think we should assume such so it lights a fire under our asses to get shit done."

Genie took another swing with the shovel, then dropped to his knees in the shallow hole. Calvin jumped in and grabbed him by the arm, knelt down. "You okay, old man?"

Genie tried to speak, but his lungs refused and spewed a cough instead, one that turned into several, then a full-fledged fit ending in more blood, which Genie tried to hide in the dirt. Finally, "Just ain't as young is all."

Calvin thought of ending the charade, telling his best friend he knew what was going on. How he remembered the exact date Genie had that doctor's appointment, and then the follow-up, where he seemed to change, like part of him had already died. Lately, Calvin wondered if zipping his lip didn't make him look like an uncaring friend or a dumbass who didn't know deep sickness when they saw it.

"Let me take this one, buddy. We've only got another foot to go. Four feet is all, remember." Calvin helped his friend up and out of the hole.

"Lunch is on me then." Genie plopped down on the grass, and his hands rested on shaky knees.

The offer of lunch made Calvin laugh, as they'd shared their income like a married couple for years now. What was his was Genie's, and vice versa.

When the grave was finished, Calvin sat on the mound of dirt, staring down into the hole.

"Wasn't for us, we wouldn't be diggin' this hole at all," Genie said.

Calvin collected Genie's thought and disposed of it like a dog turd on the sidewalk. "Wasn't for us, there might be a lot more girls out there hurtin' or in holes themselves."

Genie tried to smile but couldn't.

CHAPTER 43

THEY DIDN'T ATTEND Andy's funeral and wouldn't have even if Rosem asked. But they did catch a glimpse of the turnout, including Tim and his new knife. That devil. The turnout wasn't as many as Wendy's but enough to see the kid was loved. Enough to stir the pot of guilt that sat boiling in Genie's gut.

The two found themselves on the other end of the cemetery, quietly hand-trimming weeds and cleaning up wreaths that had rotted to the point of obscene.

"Been thinkin'," Genie said.

"Uh oh." Calvin put a bouquet of long-dead flowers in the wheelbarrow.

"We ain't had no dealings with Mallon lately. Maybe he's settled down, chalked it up as a lost battle, and decided it ain't so bad havin' a colored man around after all. Suppose we go to him, spill what Tim did to Wendy. Stress to him the deputy's got blinders on."

"Eh . . . that's a desperate move, buddy. That all you got?"

"You got something better?"

"Nope. But that one sure feels like a bad firecracker that'll go off in our faces."

As though Sheriff Mallon had somehow heard their conversation, he appeared, coming toward them with a black suit and determined gait.

"Aww, hell," Calvin whispered. "Like a demon bein' summoned."

"Well, if it ain't The Black Plague and Polio Jones. You guys roll into town and kids start dyin'. Ironic, isn't it?"

Genie took note on how much smaller the sheriff looked without his hat and belt. "Sad as hell is what it is."

"Our condolences, Sheriff." Calvin took his hat off, more out of kissing ass than respect for the dead.

"You're a bad omen, you two. I bet you've heard that before, probably from the last town that shooed your asses out."

"I don't know what to tell you, Sheriff," Genie said. "Maybe you ought look at your own for answers."

"What's that supposed to mean?" The sheriff tried hooking his thumbs into a gun belt that wasn't there, got embarrassed, fueling his ire all the more. "Boy, if I wasn't sheriff, I'd beat the tar right offa you."

"It means," Calvin said, "not everyone in this Rockwell painting of yours is a saint."

Sheriff Mallon shifted his weight, stood with a leg out. "Give me one name."

Genie and Calvin traded glances. Calvin nodded, and Genie said it. "Tim Wayne."

The sheriff seemed to freeze a moment, as though taken off guard. His mouth went from sneer to crooked line, as he fidgeted for the words to say.

"He's just a punk teen. Don't know his dick from a pinecone. But he's over there right now . . . " The sheriff pointed toward the far side of the cemetery. "With a face full of tears cuz his best friend done killed himself."

"Killed himself?" Genie said.

Calvin spoke up. "Well, there you have it. Suicide. What the hell do we have to do with it?"

The sheriff's eyes turned to slits. "One more person dies in this town, I don't care if it's Old Mother Hubbard at the age of a hundred and nine, I'll come after the both of you. You hear me?"

Genie stepped forward and stood straight, with easily four inches over Mallon. "Yeah, I hear you. But just cuz you're comin' don't mean we're backin' down. You hear *me*?"

The sheriff's lip curled until his gritting teeth showed, then he turned and walked away.

"Was that plan B? Feedin' the sharks your own leg?" Calvin said.

"May have not helped, I know. But dammit, Cal. I'm glad I said it. My self-worth blew away like wilted scales years ago. And I just snatched a piece back."

"You sure did, but I think with it came some gas for the fire."

CHAPTER 44

GENIE COULDN'T SLEEP. Digging Andy's bed, then his funeral, it had gotten to him, picking at his joy like a vulture. He switched on the small bedside lamp and wrote a long letter to Louise, scribing words he'd already said: What had happened to Andy and how exactly, then Tim. Denise and her suffering. Deputy Wayne. The asshole sheriff, which was exactly how he addressed him with each mention.

When the letter was done, he shuffled to the kitchen and helped himself to some saltines, not taking care to keep quiet, with the hope Calvin would wake and keep him company. His head was just too dark and plagued to be alone this night.

"I hear ya out there," Calvin finally mumbled from his bedroom doorway just around the corner. "What's on your mind?"

"You know." Cracker dust flew from Genie's mouth and peppered the table.

"Andy?" Calvin's voice got a little louder as he came out in a wrinkled green T-shirt and long john bottoms.

"I almost wished I'd seen what he done to that girl, right there as it happened."

"Make it a helluva lot easier, wouldn't it?" Calvin sat down, propped his elbow on the table, and leaned his head. "Wanna get some air?"

Genie nodded slowly. "Yeah, I think I do."

They didn't bother putting boots on. The night was dry and still a bit warm. The pair didn't see much grass in Chicago, so squeezing some between their toes on occasion was inviting, and there were still some scraps of September left before it'd be too cold for such a thing.

They passed a few rows of graves before Genie sighed and said, "Not sure this is helping. Ain't nothing but a constant reminder of mortality out here."

"Try and think of it as—" Then Calvin froze, gripped Genie's arm, and pointed.

There was a silhouette in the distance with a shovel in hand, digging in the ground, right around—or directly at—plot 274.

★-★-★

The men crept quietly toward the figure, who had since dropped the shovel and was now pulling things from the hole and setting them carefully in a wheelbarrow.

Genie tapped his friend on the shoulder and whispered, "The hell we scared of? We should be running at them, ready to tackle."

Calvin stopped, looked at him. "You're right." Then he took off into a full sprint, or as much of a sprint as a man his age could muster.

Genie knew he couldn't catch up, so he sent his booming voice ahead. "Hey, you! Whatchoo doin' there?!"

The figure looked up, statue still.

When Genie saw the person seemed to have no intention of running off—and Calvin was nearly there anyhow—he slowed and grabbed his chest, wheezing. The sound that came from his mouth was like sandpaper on steel. If he closed his watering eyes, he could conjure the ghostly groan of haunted house doors. He leaned forward, hands on knees, and coughed—a long, ratty thing that chewed on the way out. He dragged an arm across his lips, and even in the dim of the moonlight, he saw the oil-black smear on his dark skin.

He could see Calvin had reached the hole and appeared to be talking to the someone that was there. The figure became more than a silhouette and carried the slim figure of a grown man, not a teen like he'd suspected, out here late at night, smoking their reefer, drinking their beer, telling ghost stories. And something much more sinister, if the shovel was any indication.

Before he saw the man's features, he heard his voice and recognized it right away. It was Pastor Rosem, who'd traded his godly garb for a pair of jeans, flannel shirt, and knit cap.

"I told you before, Calvin. But I don't think you're gettin' it. These young ones, they belong in the house of God. And that's where I'm taking him."

Calvin swung around to meet Genie's wide eyes. "It's our beloved pastor, doin' the Lord's work." He said it with a layer of sarcasm thick as bread.

Genie looked at the grave and saw it'd been dug up, mounds of loose dirt surrounding it. The coffin four feet down was open and empty. The wheelbarrow was packed full of black bags that looked to be made of vinyl.

"Pastor?" Genie said. "What's going on here?" He was afraid of the answer. The pastor had been the only one in town they felt they could trust, and here he was, looking like the worst of them.

Calvin leaned into Genie. "He's been unburyin' the kids and puttin' them in the basement of the church . . . in the Lord's house, he says."

"I don't expect you boys to understand." The pastor wiped a wall of sweat from his forehead with a sleeved forearm. "This is work for a man of the cloth, and my cross to bear."

"Well, this *work* is illegal and unethical," Calvin said.

"I'm hurting no one, fellas. Now, you just go on and mind your business."

"All due respect, Pastor, but this *is* our business," Calvin said. "And you've put us in a bind. Out here desecrating graves, moving bodies."

"Now hold on." Genie walked over to the wheelbarrow and looked at the bags inside. "There something else buried in that coffin? What's this here?" He kicked at the wheelbarrow, and the bags inside shifted.

"That's poor Andy. Every piece they could find." The pastor sat on his rump and began to cry, slouched over a mound of dirt.

"Dammit all, I coulda gone without knowin' that." Genie stepped back.

"You asked," Calvin said.

While the pastor sobbed, Calvin waved Genie over and whispered, "Now what? We gonna get blamed for this too?"

Genie ran a big hand across his face. "I ain't goin' down for this. We need to go straight to the deputy, right up to his door."

"What kinda time you get for something like this?"

"I dunno. Maybe none. Maybe they'll put him on probation or in a sanitarium. I mean . . . except for this nutty shit here, he seems like his head's on straight."

Calvin called out to Rosem, "Pastor, how many bodies you got under the church?"

Rosem touched the wheelbarrow. "Precious Andy here will be eight."

"Eight? They all kids?"

"Yes, all God's children. Even Susan Bonrich's stillborn, God rest his soul."

The two went back to whisper. "Eight kids?" Genie said.

"No need to whisper, boys. I am well aware how this appears. Well aware. But I am merely a ferryman, escorting these soulless remains to a place more suited for the children of the Lord to be."

Calvin widened his eyes and looked at his friend. Genie just sighed through his nose. "Pastor. I hear your reasons, and I get it. Believe me, in a pear-shaped way it makes sense . . . but it still don't make it right. Doing wrong for right reasons don't make it so."

Genie stepped forward and looked at the bags in the wheelbarrow again. Black vinyl shining like the devil's eyes in the moonlight.

"I know that. And I know about the wages. I am prepared to take the marks against my name when the roll is called and I'm to account for it all. The Father will see my meaning and reasons and that they are pure. I will shine, boys. I will." The pastor paused and drew in a deep breath, his eyes sharpened, and he spoke again with a calmer tone. "I'm not just piling them down there like cordwood. The basement floor is unfinished, soft soil. I blessed it and interred the children to the ground. I've been cobblestoning the floor along the way. It's not a grim den, I promise."

Calvin tapped Genie on the shoulder and nodded backward, and the two stepped away from the grave again as Rosem stood and began to push the dirt back in with the flat of the shovel.

"Genie. I think we'd be best to turn our heads here. Weird and wrong as it feels, it ain't a flea bite to what else we have going on. You feelin' me?"

Genie just stared at their benefactor and the tears drying on his whiskered face as he hummed and shoveled the soil over the freshly emptied grave. He looked at Calvin and nodded. "Yeah. For now, I'd say that's the call we have to make. I'd also like to point out Jimmy Rosem ain't as crazy as he sounds. Just doesn't know how to process things. Them voices he hears . . . that's guilt. He knows what his old man's been doin', maybe even assisted a time or two. If so, probably messed him up."

Calvin tilted his head back and nodded after being given the epiphany.

Without another word, Rosem wheeled the pieces of young Andy through the shadows of the cemetery, toward the large stone square of the church. The two other men just stared and watched him go.

CHAPTER 45

GENIE SAT AT the low desk in the back of the media room of the Crownover Public Library and turned the dial on the side of the microfiche machine. He was careful not to go too quickly or he'd make himself seasick again, so he slowly scrolled through the yellow stills of the local paper, going six years back. He stopped when he saw the headline about a house fire. He read the short article. How Mel Turner, who had only recently lost his wife to cancer, had perished in the flames. How the investigation led them to believe it was an accident, that Mel had fallen asleep with a cigarette lit and burned the house down with him in its belly. Their young son, Tim, the only survivor, as he had been staying the night at his uncle's house, Jeremy Wayne. There was a grainy photo of a slightly younger Deputy Wayne.

Genie sat up straight and rolled his shoulders, his neck popping audibly. He looked around the dim room and saw no other people but Calvin, who sat at the longer table flipping through a music magazine. He read the last line about how Sheriff Mallon was the first on the scene and had made several attempts to stall entry for safety's sake, until the house was mostly gutted by hungry flames.

"Cal," Genie whispered, "got something pertinent here. Seems like the scuttlebutt we heard wasn't far off."

Calvin got up and walked slowly to where his friend waited. The librarian at the big desk watched him over the top of her glasses. Calvin winked at her, and she looked down at her book. "Whatcha got, Sherlock?" Calvin said.

"See for yourself." Genie leaned aside and let his pal have a view of the screen. Calvin's lips moved as he read. Genie looked over to the desk lady and gave her a smile she did not return.

The two walked out of the library.

"Well, that's some sad shit." Calvin shivered as his body recalibrated from the coolness of the library to the late summer warmth.

"It is. And . . . not being sympathetic, but that'd definitely twist a boy. Losing his mama, then dad, and then finding out the circumstances behind it. Unless, of course, his perversions started long before he lost his parents. Said in there Tim was at his uncle's house, stayin' the night, when the fire went down. The little asshole could have already been startin' his bullshit."

Genie's response was cut short by a car horn close by. They both turned to see Deputy Wayne and Tim sitting at the opposite side of the intersection in Wayne's cruiser. Wayne waved at them and gave a big smile. The smirkish grin on the boy's face was dark and barbed as a scorpion's tale.

They kept watching as the cruiser turned and shrank down the street. The dregs of whatever small sympathies they may have been holding trickled through their fingers.

"One thing's for sure," Genie said. "Tim ain't talkin'. He's layin' low. Mallon called Andy's death a suicide. Tim knows that ain't true, which means he ain't comin' after us. Cuz if he does, he'll have to explain why he never said nothin' when the word suicide was bein' thrown around."

"The thing is, I don't know that Mallon cares to think that deep if he knows he can lay it on us."

Genie shook his head and sighed. "This ain't what we signed up for, Cal. Hell, we had less drama in the Windy City."

"You ain't kiddin'. But if our speculation is correct about Tim's dad and Mallon, we might have the same leverage on the sheriff the deputy does. And we may just have to use it."

"And if he calls our bluff?" Genie looked at his friend through worried eyes.

"We're on the first train out of here."

CHAPTER 46

THE TWO SPENT the rest of the day working the grounds, which included tidying up Andy's grave. There was talk on whether or not they were doing the right thing by looking the other way, but ultimately bad timing being a major factor settled it. There was just too much bullshit to contend with, and like Calvin had said, Pastor Rosem's soul-snatching paranoia was nothing in comparison.

They saw Denise in the distance, tracing a gravestone. They waved, and she waved back. She'd done well keeping her distance, but seeing her was a reminder that so far they'd done less than shit to help her.

Calvin broke a dead branch free from a pine tree and tossed it in the wheelbarrow. "What if we get Denise to agree to a public confrontation? Like one Sunday morning, she confronts Tim with everything right in front of the whole congregation. And we'll be there for backup and to spill our own about Wendy on the train."

Genie adjusted the leather glove on his hand where his pinkie poked through. He thought on Calvin's words a moment. "That might work if Denise was a grown woman and could handle such a scene. But I don't know she'd feel comfortable letting the whole town gawk while she pulls them skeletons out." He looked over at the girl again, and his mouth wilted.

"What would Jim Rockford do?"

Genie chuckled. "For $200 a day plus expenses? A whole helluva lot more than what we're capable of."

"He'd also manage to get himself some tail while he's at it."

Genie could only offer a weak smile that starved on its way across as he thought of Louise.

Calvin seemed to catch on. "Hell, maybe we're too old anyway. We've had our fair share."

"You think Louise misses me?" Genie stopped hunting for dead twigs and leaned against the tree. His breath came heavier than it should and held a raspy wheeze in its thin fingers.

Calvin looked at his friend for a long, quiet moment before answering. "I'm sure she thinks of you often, Genie. I've no doubt."

Genie tried to bury his frown behind a melodic whistle as he worked, the sound weak and barely audible from a set of dying lungs.

CHAPTER 47

THE DAY HAD brought aching bones and sore feet, and by the time dark began to fall, the only thing on their mind was food. Heading to Loretta's Lunchbox was an easy choice to make.

"First payday, I'm thinking we stock the cupboards. Hitting the church for the free meal is fine. But comin' here instead, I can see a habit forming that'll burn another hole in our pockets if we're not careful." Genie said it, but it's not what he wanted. He didn't necessarily like eating in their tiny home. Privacy and solitude was something he grew less fond of as his sickness progressed. There was something about being in the midst of shiny faces that made him feel less alone. He'd learned a long time ago that happiness was a contagion. And so was lament. Spend too much time wallowing and the grave would come sooner than it should. Laughter was the best medicine. So was the smokescreen of good spirits and the crow's feet from a toothy smile.

"And save the money for what? You gonna get yourself a muscle car?"

"Yeah . . . make you a nice bed in the trunk. While all the tail I get sits up front with me."

"Shiiit," Calvin said. They chuckled low.

Genie ordered meatloaf with mac and cheese and an extra cup of gravy. Calvin got the spaghetti with toast but no garlic. They both ordered milk.

While they were waiting on their food, Genie said, "You'll think I'm crazy, but I miss the donut holes from Joe & Dough's. Even the ones from the dumpster."

"Make for a nice dessert. Don't miss fetching 'em, though. I ever tell you about the morning I had to all but wrestle that rat the size of a beagle?"

"I've heard that tall tale a few times, yes." Genie sipped on his glass of milk, then coughed into his sleeve. The fit started slow, then progressed into one of the worst he'd had. By the time he was done, the stark white napkin from his lap was peppered in crimson. There was no hiding it, and the elephant in the room may as well been polka-dotted too, with a raging hard-on.

Calvin looked away, probably feigning that he hadn't seen a thing.

After wiping his mouth and balling up the napkin, Genie let out a long, deep sigh, prepping for confession. "Cal . . . "

Calvin looked at him with a tight smile and warm eyes.

"I got the cancer . . . " Genie tapped his chest with two fingers. "Right here."

Calvin reached out and grabbed his friend's large hand in both of his. "I know."

Genie's posture changed. He sat up straight. "You know? I been talkin' in my sleep again?"

"I got a confession of my own to make. That last appointment you had down at the VA . . . well, you ain't been the same since. I knew something was wrong . . . so I peeked at that cursed reminder you keep in your pocket. I'm sorry." A tear rolled down the old man's face. "I'm just . . . so sorry."

"Sounds like something you'd do."

"I didn't say anything because I knew you would on your own time."

"Is that why you pushed for us to have this last adventure?" Genie cocked an eyebrow.

"Maybe. But this ain't the last one."

"You know something I don't?"

"Holding out hope, I guess."

"The coughing . . . that's the part you can see. Maybe the wear and tired, too. But, friend, I can feel the rot inside, and it's gotten downright unbearable the past few weeks. I don't know how much longer I can hold on."

Calvin kept silent, lending a wide-open ear and a dry shoulder. He squeezed his friend's hand.

"I've been keeping everything but the coughs back. Those are like holding in a sneeze with a nose full of pepper. The pain inside, the feelin' like I'm runnin' through honey with a sack of shit on my back, I've kept that to myself."

The waitress brought their food, but the desire for a full belly had waned. After she left, Calvin said, "I'm sorry, Genie. I wish I'd said something a long time ago. Nobody should go through something like this alone, especially you. You've been through enough. I should have been there."

Genie waved a hand. "You *have* been there, and if I'm honest, I had a sneaking suspicion you were onto me. It didn't add up that you never asked how I was. It's more like you to slap me with questions if you so much as see a new gray hair on my head."

This made Calvin smile. Genie too. Finally, they ate their food, scraping every bit from the plate, then ordered vanilla pudding with wafers for dessert. A favorite of both.

CHAPTER 48

SHERIFF MALLON WAS parked down the street, assuming the position with his one arm resting on the door. Through the dark, the two men could just make out the pale shape of a cup of coffee in his hand and the glare in his eyes, as he watched them—his new favorite pastime.

They took the long way home, which was along the fence where Wendy Birdsong's grave was. This path had become routine, either because of familiarity or their way of paying continual respects to the poor girl, Calvin wasn't sure—even though she wasn't actually in the grave but underneath the church, where Pastor Rosem prayed over eight different kids on the daily.

"Do we even want to stay here?" Calvin said as they passed the grave. "It ain't the Mayberry we thought it was. And it seems the longer we stay, the more shit sticks to our heels."

"It ain't in me to hop a train again, Cal. Now that you know I got the sick, I'm okay with sayin' I'm going nowhere. This is home 'til the end." He stopped and pointed toward the far corner of the cemetery where the stones couldn't be seen, only the silhouette of pine limbs cast from a streetlight overhead. "Matter of fact, I like that plot right over there, like a spotlight shining down on me."

"Bullshit, Genie. Stop it with the grim—"

"Plot 138. That's what I want . . . an' if you don't visit me twice a day and three times on Sunday, I will definitely be haunting your old ass."

Calvin shook his head and felt the lump in his throat, like his own tumor eating away at the toughened muscle in his chest. It couldn't wait to throw him to his knees, where he'd beg God for strength to go on without his best friend.

"Bullshit," Calvin mumbled under his breath so Genie couldn't hear and wiped away the tear that teetered on his lid.

As the two climbed the small hill toward the cottage, Genie nodded up ahead. "You leave the light on?"

Calvin swung his eyes from the ground to see the cottage windows lit in amber. "Probably." His pace quickened. Genie kept his slower gait and followed. He was only three steps behind when Calvin threw open the door.

"Evening, fellas." The voice was not that of Pastor Rosem or the sheriff or Deputy Wayne, nor was it Denise. The less-than-six-foot silhouette hung back from the table so the light threw them in shadow.

"Who's there?" Genie mumbled as he squinted tired eyes.

"You know damn well who it is." The intruder took a step around the table and began to reveal himself in the fan of light from the lamp's shaded bulb.

The hostility told Genie it was Sheriff Mallon, but the tenor of the voice still said otherwise.

"And I bet you can figure out why, too . . . " The face that came into view was a young one. Sharp and thin. Ratty eyes that glistened like wet glass. The mouth in perpetual sneer. Tim Wayne stood in their parlor. And as the light continued to peck at the shadows, they saw he was holding a gun.

Calvin felt his skin chill, every hair rising at attention. He stole a look at his friend and saw Genie wore a mask the mixture of rage and terror.

"We need to talk." Tim motioned to the table and chairs with the nose of the pistol. "Sit down."

Calvin pulled out his usual chair and Genie his. They stared at the boy who appeared to be holding their future in a shaky hand. Up close, they could see he was sweating and jumpy. Not the demeanor of a hardened killer. He was as terrified as they were, with one major difference: Tim Wayne was out of his head.

"What's on your mind, Tim?" How Genie managed to sound so calm was a feat of pure magic.

Calvin just stared at the bigger man, incredulous.

Tim paced in the small area on his side of the table, never taking his eyes off the men.

"I wanna say first that Wendy was an accident. I know you probably don't believe that, but it's true. Shit got outta hand, that's all." The kid tried to smile, but it faded quickly. "I want you guys out of here. Pack whatever hobo shit you have and blow away. You do that and things will be okay. You stick around, and well . . . not so much."

Genie felt heat rising through his muscles and chest. He let out a deep breath through flared nostrils and looked hard into the kid's eyes. "We're done here. I got nothin' to lose, and I'm damn sure not gonna be bullied by a rattail rapist, murdering fucker like you." Genie made to stand, and Tim raised the gun, the end of the barrel mere feet from the black man's face.

"Nope. Sit down or I'll shoot you and your white shadow here." He looked Genie right in the eye and that fishhook sneer caught tight.

Genie glanced at Calvin and saw him staring behind Tim, at the open window above the desk. Genie's eyes followed and thought he saw movement in the folds of night beyond the window. He felt the breeze coming in through the screen.

Lord, let that be the cavalry a comin'.

"I mean it. I want you gone tonight. Go back to where you came from or keep heading west and jump in the ocean. I don't give a shit, just so long as you're gone. And don't forget who my uncle is. Going to the law ain't gonna help. I'm the son he never had."

The boy stopped ranting, and the room was quiet. Only the sound of leaves whispering in the slight wind floated in from outside.

Then Tim jerked his arm, tightening his grip on the gun. "Pack your shit and be quick with it. Move! Now!"

***

Genie put his hands over his face, closed his eyes. Quietly, lower than a whisper, he asked for guidance and strength and some kinda way out of this. He was coming up on Amen when the butt of the pistol connected with his head. He tried to move from receiving the second blow but fell off his chair, onto weak knees. His right ear burned as a wet stream tickled the skin of his neck.

"You fucking deaf, old man? Get moving."

Genie nodded and saw the dark-red droplets of his blood on the floor. He gripped the edge of the table and made to pull himself up. Outside the window, a *click*. Tim turned toward the screen, and Calvin nodded to Genie, then flipped the table up and rushed the boy. Genie scrambled to his feet and helped, pushing the small but solid table into Tim's chest.

Tim stumbled back and into the wall. The gun fell from his hand, landing in front of the stove. Calvin continued the push, pinning Tim against the wall, while Genie went for the gun and brought it to the boy's nose.

"Now who says what?" Genie breathed the words hard into Tim's face, nose to nose, while pressing his weight against the table. Tim gasped, face burning red, eyes bulging.

"Get the cops, Cal," Genie managed through a cough. "I got this little shit."

Calvin let the table go and took a step back, letting his friend handle it. The door swung open, and Deputy Wayne stepped in, his service pistol in hand. "The cops are right here." He surveyed the room and looked at the brick-red face of his nephew against the wall. "Let him out."

"Deputy Wayne, you don't understand . . . "

"Oh, I understand damn well. I've been outside that window for the last ten minutes." He gave his nephew a hardened frown.

Genie let the table fall and stepped away, then the overexertion hit him, as sudden lethargy gripped his legs. He dropped to his knees.

"Eugene, slide that gun over here before you get yourself in trouble," the deputy said.

Genie complied.

"He needs a doctor," Calvin said, then kneeled down and looked over his friend's head wound.

"First thing's first," the deputy said, the gun still out and pointing toward all three. "What'd you do to Wendy Birdsong, boy?"

Genie let out a sigh of relief and held his bleeding head in shaky hands.

"It was an accident, Uncle Jeremy. We were on the train, just messin' around." The boy's voice cracked, his face breaking into painful grooves meant to bring tears.

"Bullshit! What you did was no accident. I saw that poor girl lying there, naked, legs spread after you and your buddy finished with her," Calvin said.

The deputy tilted his head. The bones in his neck cracked loudly. "Is that why Andy killed himself?"

Tim swallowed hard, then nodded at the two men huddled on the ground in front of him. "They killed him. They threw him from the train, and they threw me too. My sprained ankle? I didn't get that playin' ball. I got it from them trying to kill me."

"Hold on just a second, boy." Calvin put a hand up. "Deputy, those boys tried pushing us off the train on account of what they'd done. We were witnesses. Loose ends. That's how it really went down. It was all self-defense."

"They're lyin', Uncle Jeremy."

The deputy's eyes darted back and forth between the two. "Okay, I've heard enough."

"How about you tell your uncle about diddling his dau—"

"I said enough!" Deputy Wayne extended his arm, pointed it straight at Calvin. "Now, this doesn't mean I don't like you fellas, but blood's thicker and runs deeper."

Genie lifted his weary head. "You gotta be kidding me. How 'bout your own daughter? That boy's been messin' with her."

Somehow, Tim's face grew a deeper shade of red before saying, "They're full of shit, Uncle Jeremy! It's just crazy, senile talk . . . like Jimmy Rosem. You can't believe a word they're saying."

The deputy gave a heavy sigh as he aimed the gun at Genie. "I can't lose that boy. No matter what he's done, *I* will sort it. He's my responsibility."

Calvin looked at Genie, an expression that said the cop's cheese was far off his cracker.

"You're raising a pervert, Deputy." Genie looked at Tim, eyes drilling through him.

"Okay . . . " the deputy started. "I think it's best you fellas move along now. We don't need more shit-stirring here in Crownover. You didn't come in with much, you won't leave with much. No reason to pack, just start walking. I'll give you a ride to the depot, and you'll hop on a train and not show your face here again." He glared at his nephew with a profoundly wounded look and a slight shake of his head. "Boy, you come along. I ain't letting you out of my sight." His voice had an edge to it that seemed to unnerve the kid. Tim paled and nodded.

"Let's go." Deputy Wayne jerked the gun toward the door, and the men shambled out in front of him, Tim following Calvin, and the deputy bringing up the rear. The door remained ajar as they made their way into the dark cemetery.

CHAPTER 49

THE NIGHT AIR had dropped in degrees, but the old men were soaked in nervous sweat. They rode in the back of the patrol car, Tim in the front with his uncle. Other than the occasional sniffle from Tim, the car was quiet.

Calvin watched the buildings fly by, saying silent goodbyes to the cemetery grounds, the church, Loretta's Lunchbox and its empty picnic tables. Being continually removed from where you lay your head was something that would never fail to break Calvin's heart. But this time things were different. His best friend was dying. It trumped every other time they'd been told to move along, shoved from a park bench, evicted from under the bridge, having their tent lit on fire while out scrounging for change to ease the pangs that clawed at their empty bellies.

Genie leaned against the car door, head in his hands, blood drying in rust-colored streams down his fingers.

"Deputy . . . Genie needs a doctor. I think he's got a concussion."

"He's a big boy. He'll be fine," was all the deputy said, but it sounded like there may have been a sliver of remorse nested in it.

After a ride much shorter than anticipated, the deputy pulled over. Calvin recognized the terrain.

The driver's side door opened, and Deputy Wayne stepped out. The gun had returned to his hand. "Open the door for Mr. Eugene, Tim."

The boy got out and did as he was told, while the deputy opened the other door for Calvin. As he waited for the two men to get out, Wayne surveyed the surrounding wooded area, the hills, the field, as though searching for potential witnesses to the eviction. The fact they were still within city limits and nowhere near a depot worried Calvin.

"Up this way." The deputy pointed toward a trail, the same trail Sheriff Mallon brought them through. Genie's stomach dropped like a runaway elevator.

··*·

Genie and Calvin walked almost shoulder to shoulder, Genie occasionally losing a step and using Calvin to stay on his feet. The deputy shuffled behind, close enough his breath danced on their necks, his gun raised and steady, ready to bark and halt at any moment. Tim brought up the rear, a few steps to the side of his uncle, sobbing quietly.

"Shoulda listened to our guts and hauled ass days ago," Calvin whispered from the side of his mouth.

"You fellas keep quiet. I got a head full of hornets, and I'm trying to sort it. I don't need your noise. Your sniveling either, boy. Shit, this wouldn't even be happening if it weren't for you." The man's voice cracked on the last part, the depth of his hurt and disappointment on rickety display.

They walked on in awkward silence, until the town petered out, obscured by trees and high grass. Genie saw the *Welcome to Crownover* sign, and his stomach somersaulted when Wayne told them which path to take as it veered deeper. The eerie sense of deja vu was nothing supernatural here. They had most definitely been on this path before.

They found their steps shuffling and short, as though their ankles were shackled together. Genie looked back at Tim and saw the boy's face shining with tears, his lips moving as if he was delivering a silent litany. The look on Deputy Wayne's face was terrifying. A cowl of dark desire webbed his features.

"Let's get a hoof on, fellas," Wayne spoke in a clipped manner, but the stern authority was clear.

The path opened into an area where the grasses and weeds were flattened and the dilapidated remains of a building stood. Genie stopped and looked to Calvin, then they both turned their attention to the shack where they had spent most of their first night in town, until being unpleasantly roused by Sheriff Mallon, starting them on the trajectory that now seemed close to an end.

Genie breathed heavily and looked back at Calvin. The smaller man's face was thin with worry. Genie nodded, his own eyes puffy and tired, the blood on his head and neck, drying and caked.

"Come on, boys. Head inside." The sheriff waved the pistol toward the dilapidated door.

The old men made their way into the dark mouth of the derelict building and stood in the same spot where they'd slept that night. They stared at their feet while waiting for the deputy and Tim to enter.

Genie had a good understanding of how this would end. Shallow graves, nowhere near Kimball Pines Cemetery. They were not being led to the edge of town. This was the end of days. The last page in the final adventure. They'd push the daisies here in the field, trampled underfoot by generations of children eager to make the old shed their new clubhouse.

He looked at his friend. Calvin was staring straight ahead, into the shadows, waiting for the bullet. Genie took the orange scarf Louise had made him and draped it over his friend's shoulders. "I'll take this exit over rotting from the cancer. But you . . . " He could barely get the words out. "You've got a lotta years left, old man. A lotta years." Genie's tears sparkled liked diamonds in a weathered wall of coal.

Calvin's nostrils flared as he held back his own tears, still staring ahead, as though taking a goodbye glance at his best friend would break him in two.

Wayne's voice came from behind them. "I take no pleasure in this . . . just so you know. But it looks like Andy's death is on you, so this here is your sentence."

"And Denise?" Calvin spoke it loud and clear. His eyes were steely and his jaw set. He expected a bullet to the face for his audacity.

Wayne's gaze back was a sharpened sword, and Calvin cowered under the gleam of it. "I told you I'd handle it." He turned and pushed his nephew back through the doorway and into the night.

The two aging men stood there, trying to hear the words spoken outside. They could hear the deputy's wavering voice but not the words that were said. The words they *could* hear were from Tim's mouth, whimpering that'd he'd only been curious about Denise and her body and that he meant no harm.

Calvin watched the deputy's silhouette as it extended an arm and turned its head away.

"Uncle Jeremy! I'm sorr—"

A gunshot exploded, and the men started, then froze.

Genie felt his bladder threaten to release, his legs weaker than ever. Calvin gripped his arm like a mother to her wobbling toddler, holding him in place.

Deputy Wayne stumbled through the doorway, his face wet with tears, his chest heaving. A thin snake of smoke still floated from the nose of the gun in his hand.

"Dear Lord," Genie muttered.

"You shouldn't have done that," the deputy growled. "Put the gun down, Eugene!"

Confusion formed on Genie's face. "I ain't got no—"

The deputy pointed the gun at his own foot and pulled the trigger. A ragged hole appeared in the leather over the toe. Blood and a glimpse of pale bone filled the space.

"Sonofabitch!" The deputy hopped on one leg, dragging a clawed hand up his calf. "Fuuuck!" He raised the gun on the men. "You shot me, Eugene. And you shot my boy. You're gonna die for that." Eyes on Calvin now. "You both stay right where you are. Calvin, stop!"

Genie understood. The deputy was staging a struggle, covering his ass. But the black man had no fight left in him. His head swam dizzily from the knock to the head, and the thought of being an invalid due to his blackened lungs, with Calvin playing caretaker, he was ready. "I'll see you soon, Louise," he whispered.

A new booming voice followed his own. "Put the gun down, Jeremy!"

Until now, Genie had hated that voice.

Sheriff Mallon stood just outside the shed-house, his service gun gripped with both hands, finger on the trigger and pointed at Deputy Wayne.

Without turning, Deputy Wayne said, "You do like the deep end, don't you, Mallon?" His voice was something heaved in breathy chunks.

"You can spill every word you think you've got on me, but I'll not have you committing murder in my town. Now put the gun down, or I'll put a bullet in your back."

"Sounds about right, killin' men when their back is turned." Wayne brought his other hand up to steady the gun.

While Genie was ready to fly with the angels only a moment before, the sudden prospect of not dying this day flicked a switch. Not so much for himself but for his friend, who was not ready to leave the earth. There was a little fight in him after all.

Calvin slowly craned his neck, trying to read what might come next.

"I'm counting to three, Jeremy. Then this barrel gets hot."

CHAPTER 50

MALLON SEEMED TO key into whatever Genie had been thinking, as the synchronicity seemed otherworldly. The sheriff stepped fully into the room and ducked low at the same moment Genie lunged forward and swung a thick arm across the short space, connecting with the deputy's throat.

Wayne's eyes went wide, and he raised the gun, pulled the trigger. The noise was like God stomping on a tin roof.

Calvin screamed and joined in the chaos. Genie was on the floor, holding his now-ringing ear, his breathing heavy and ragged. He managed to get himself to his knees as Wayne pointed the gun down at the gray wooly hair on the old man's head.

Calvin rushed forward, raised a foot, and brought it down with all the force he could muster on the deputy's wounded one. The man howled like a demon, yet he held onto the gun. Swung it upward, right in Calvin's face. There was another bang.

Everything in the small room went still. Except for Deputy Wayne, who crashed to the floor in a tangled heap.

Genie looked up first, expecting to see his friend had made it to the grave before him, but Calvin was standing, eyes on Mallon and the gun in his hand.

Mallon was very matter-of-fact when he spoke. "I'm gonna need you to stay right here. We got a real mess on our hands. *I* know what happened, but the state boys are gonna wanna hear it from you."

Genie grabbed his head as a sharp pain drove through it.

"On second thought, we'll get you to the hospital. They can do their chatting there."

"No . . . no doctor. No hospital," Genie said and held back vomit that was begging to come up.

"Genie . . . you might have a concussion. You're goin'." Calvin's voice was pleading.

Genie's eyes turned to slits as he looked up at his friend. "I ain't goin'."

While the vomit stayed put, a cough came forward, followed by another, stretching into a long succession that sounded more like seals choking on sawdust.

"Your friend's right. You're in bad shape." Mallon holstered his gun. "It'd be best if you went."

"Well, then you're gonna have to drag my ass there in cuffs, Sheriff."

Calvin shrugged, raised his brow at the sheriff. "Yeah, he ain't goin'." Looked back at Genie. "Stubborn ass."

Mallon shook his head. "I need to go radio this in." He suddenly looked tired and not at all like the monster the men had seen up until now. Just a man with a lot going on in the cage of his mind. "Keep that fool sitting." He nodded at Genie.

They watched the man's shadow become one with the darkness outside, until he was out of sight. Genie stood on wobbly legs, and Calvin hooked his arm under that of his friend as they made their way to the open front door.

The body of Tim Wayne lay on its side, one arm extended above the ruins of his head. The bullet had either entered or exited through his left eye. There were still strings of steam rising from the rugged fissure into the cool air.

"Don't feel at all like I thought it might," Genie mumbled.

"How's that? Like comeuppance? Shit, secret wishin' or even out in front wishin' for something bad to befall a person, even deserved . . . that doesn't ever feel better than the crown of thorns it is, brother." Calvin squeezed his friend's arm and sighed. "It's a tragedy, especially for Denise."

Genie's eyes widened a little, as though he hadn't realized until now how this outcome would affect her. He allowed a tear to fall and sniffed the rest back when he saw the shadowy form of Mallon making its way up the path.

CHAPTER 51

BACK AT THE Crownover Police Station, the men were pummeled with questions, while Sheriff Mallon received the same treatment in another room. Most questions were asked more than once. No stone left unturned. A cop had died. A boy had died. The dead cop accused of slaying his own nephew. Every piece had to fit.

Genie and Calvin kept silent about anything that led up to the execution of Tim Wayne and the subsequent karma that dug a dime-sized hole in the deputy's back. They gave no allusion to the struggle on the train, the rape and death of Wendy Birdsong, Denise and her cousin's nighttime visits, or even Pastor Rosem's graverobbing baptisms. Both men knew the last person a cop wanted to blame for a murder was another cop, or cop kin. If the men let on they'd been on that train with the dead girl and not said a word, the state may try and fit the same broken pieces together they feared Mallon would, mashing what wouldn't fit just so they could hang the finished thing on the wall and call it a masterwork.

Two hours later, the men were free to go. Sheriff Mallon volunteered to provide the ride, and as they walked toward his patrol car, Genie hurled in the grass, head still spinning from the beating he'd taken. The smell of the bile was acrid and barbed, gouging the air around them. Calvin had to help carry him the rest of the way to the car, as Genie coughed weakly, lips wet with blood.

"If you don't let me take you to the hospital, you're dumber than I thought," Mallon said.

"He ain't lying, you know?" Calvin whispered so only Genie could hear.

Genie glared at the sheriff. "I'll be a new man tomorrow."

The three got in the car without another word and sat in silence as the radio buzzed on low like a hornet's nest trapped in the dashboard. They didn't thank Mallon for saving their lives. Genie knew it was pride that stopped him, but he still couldn't figure Mallon out, if what Jimmy Rosem said was true—the sheriff in love with a black woman.

Mallon cocked his head toward them a few times, like he was about to say something, only to sigh softly and return his attention to the road.

The men gazed out the back window of the cruiser as it slid down the street toward the church-end of town. Several of the houses on the street had bright windows, like excited eyes, while inside, people waited with anxious ears to hear all about the drama that'd unfolded.

The car made the turn into Kimball Pines Cemetery and up the hill, where they spotted the parsonage light on and made out the silhouette of Pastor Rosem on the porch.

CHAPTER 52

THE CAR IDLED outside the cottage, the headlights off. Sheriff Mallon sat in the front seat and stared ahead while Genie and Calvin waited for him to unlock the doors and let them scurry. Genie was breathing heavier than usual, and it sounded like someone filing metal. Calvin winced and side-eyed his friend. Genie had his eyes closed, and his lips moved almost imperceptibly. Perhaps praying.

Sheriff Mallon sat quiet and still, as though waiting for the courage to say something on his mind or for his pride to leave long enough to offer at least a few appropriate words.

The pride seemed to break. "Sorry you had to witness all that," was all he said, then got out of the car and opened the doors for the men. Calvin nodded and wasted no time leading Genie into their small home that wasn't quite as inviting as it once was.

Calvin took Genie to his bed, laid him down, and unlaced his boots. The soft pebble crunch of the sheriff's car tires announced his slow departure.

"The hell you doin', Genie?" Calvin sat on the edge of the bed, tugging at one of Genie's boots.

"Waitin' to see if you're gonna feed me with an airplane spoon, maybe toss a diaper on my ass." Genie's eyes were shut tight as he spoke.

"You should be in the hospital. Ain't no doubt you've got a concussion."

"Nothing a little sleep can't fix." Genie coughed as he said it, and though his build was big, the weakness in the effort made him appear much smaller. Frail and half dead.

"Sleep is exactly what you don't want. Now, sit the hell up."

"Head pounds too much when I'm up. Just gimme a minute. I need to close my eyes."

Calvin dropped the boot to the floor and sat there holding his best friend's damp foot as Genie began to softly snore. Calvin watched him, knowing that what he was standing guard against was a thing he'd not see. Like a thief in the night, as they said.

He held Genie's foot and listened hard to his breathing, while in his heart offering prayers of his own.

··*

Genie woke with a startling cough he muffled with the pillow, but the nausea came again, and he turned his head, releasing what was left in his belly onto the floor.

He pushed himself from the bed and stood on rubber knees, then shuffled out of his room and down the short hall to peek at the clock. He'd only been asleep for an hour, and it'd done absolutely nothing for the jackhammer in his head. If anything, it was worse. And the hearing in his left ear was nothing but a high-pitched squeal, like a panicked mouse burrowed deep inside him. His entire body ached, as though he'd fallen down a hill peppered with rocks. Every joint hurt, skin tender to the touch. Wet paper trying to bear the weight of stones. Some of it was from the assault, some from age, and some, he knew for sure, from the cancer.

He downed a glass of water, walked back down the hall and to his room, being careful not to wake Calvin, who seemed to be deep in the belly of sleep.

The aching man pulled his pen and paper from off the milk crates he'd been using as a nightstand and lay on his side on the bed. He wrote Louise's name at the top of a fresh sheet of paper, then let the words flow, wetting the page with tears as he did so. Before he wrote the obligatory "Love yours truly, Eugene" at the bottom, he drifted off.

CHAPTER 53

CALVIN WOKE TO the sun in his eyes. As fall approached, a few of the surrounding trees surrendered their foliage early, leaving gaps where a natural curtain once hung high above.

He squinted, rubbed the stubble on his face and the sleep from his eyes. Other than the birds, the cottage was quiet. Peaceful. He rose, planted his feet on the floor, and felt the cool, hard wood underneath them. "If you haven't already made it, I'll take a cup now."

There came no reply. Calvin had briefly forgotten about the night before. If anyone was entitled to sleep in today, it was Genie. "Never mind," he mumbled. "I'll get it."

He stood, stretched his back, and fetched the socks that lay in a ball near the bed. They'd reached the stage where they may as well be moccasins now, the soles of them hardened with a thin layer of grime.

Calvin could see Genie's legs, lying on his side, his right hand holding the pen he wrote so many letters to Louise with. There was something about the way the pen sat in his friend's open hand that Calvin didn't like. His skin turned cold, heart fluttered. Nostrils wide with a long, deep breath. He knew before he crept into the hall and saw Genie's slack jaw and crusted chin. Before he smelled the shit in Genie's pants and the deafening silence of no sound at all, not even the quiet rumble of cancerous breath maintaining life.

"Genie . . . ?" Calvin's voice cracked, eyes bubbled with saline. "Genie . . . get up, you lazy bastard. You stubborn old man . . . wake up!" The words rode on a wave of dried husks and brittle twigs that went unheard. "Eugene MacDowell . . . you've got letters to write and work that needs doing." Calvin dropped to his knees there in the hallway and buried his face in calloused hands. Howls of grief filled the old parsonage as he wept. "I can't do this on my own, Genie . . . I just can't."

Had Genie been alive, he'd cock his head at the man on the floor, having never seen him in this state. When they'd met, Calvin's heart had already been broken and mostly mended. On the inside, he was the tougher of the two. Seeing no less of hell than Genie, but the walls stood stronger. And yet here Calvin was, putting to shame any anguish Genie had ever expressed.

Calvin cried until his head filled with pounding hammers and rolling boulders. Then he cried some more.

CHAPTER 54

CALVIN SAT AT the kitchen table across from an empty chair, while Sheriff Mallon, Pastor Rosem, and two other men helped carry Eugene MacDowell out on a gurney, a crisp white sheet hiding the gentle giant beneath. Calvin didn't watch. He stared at the spot where Genie used to sit, writing useless letters to a woman who'd been dead for two years—an angel he refused to let go.

Outside, the coroner's van door shut, breaking Calvin from his trance. Pastor Rosem walked back inside, rested a hand on the seated man's shoulder. "I want you to know expenses are taken care of, Calvin."

Calvin made to thank the man, meaning to speak his gratitude for everything he'd done for them. But when he opened his mouth, only the dry whisper of *"Plot one-thirty-eight"* barely found its way to the pastor's ear.

Rosem squeezed Calvin's shoulder and nodded.

Sheriff Mallon entered and spoke softly to the pastor. Calvin heard random words, but nothing settled enough to register. It was all static, errant noise filling the giant empty silence left by his friend. His brother. He looked at the pen on the table before him, laid his hand on it, and found there were still more tears to come.

CHAPTER 55

CALVIN SPENT MOST of the day in bed. Fatigue squeezed him like the coils of a snake. He'd open his eyes and intend to rise, to do something, anything, then close them again and drift off. This went on the remainder of the day.

It was the next morning when he finally felt as though he could move. He sat on the edge of the bed and watched the motes of dust float in the rays of feeble sunlight that reached through the window. He nearly yelled for Genie before remembering, then hung his head, realizing that was no nightmare. This was real life.

In the kitchen, he'd just filled the pot of water for the stove when he heard the noise outside. A metallic clink and hushed voices. He frowned and stepped to the window, his nose touching the cool glass. Pastor Rosem and a bigger man were leading a wheelbarrow full of shovels across the cemetery grounds toward the spot his dear friend had picked for his own.

Calvin's heart ached as he watched, knowing they meant to prepare Genie's bed. He went back to his room and fetched his boots.

✻✻✻

As Calvin drew closer to plot 138, he could see the other man with the pastor was Mallon in plain clothes. He'd already broke the earth with a shovel and was tossing the first clump of grass aside.

Calvin quietly cleared his throat and said, "While I don't want to seem ungrateful, this is my job, fellas."

Pastor Rosem waved a hand. "Calvin, you go on home and rest. We've got this." The pastor spoke with a warmth of honesty that made Calvin smile somewhere inside, even if the man was a graverobbing loon.

"Okay, let me rephrase that. I need to do this." Calvin reached a hand toward the sheriff. Mallon stared at the older man, and after they played that game a few moments, he reluctantly handed over the shovel.

Calvin drove the tool into the earth and peeled back the lush green. "I'll be making this a six-footer, pastor."

Pastor Rosem shot sketchy eyes at the sheriff. "Yes, of course . . . as always. Six feet." If the sheriff smelled suspicion in the air, he said nothing. "Well, I guess we'll leave you alone then. Again, I'm sorry, Calvin. Genie was a great man. I'm blessed to have met him."

The sheriff nodded, and the two men turned and walked away.

As Calvin lined his friend's grave with a thick, brown border of dirt, he figured this would be the last grave he ever dug. The familiarity of Chicago seemed to call his name with its ragged voice. Back there, he may have not known where each meal would come, but he knew the spots from which to pluck it. Chicago didn't wear a cloak that hid the warts like Crownover did. She was an honest bitch who told it like it was. Yes, the poison here in town had been diluted, but he still kept his shoulder cold when it came to Mallon and his racist ass. Genie may have eventually forgiven him, but Calvin wasn't ready for that.

**

Hours went by. Calvin's arms burned with an ache he hadn't felt in years. Not since basic training, when he was a sliver of the man he'd become. Sweat soaked his shirt and the crack of his ass. Dirt tickled his eyes, and the open blisters that'd formed on the insides of his hands were hard to ignore any longer, as the sweat stung the pink skin with its salt.

"Looks like you could use a break."

Calvin hadn't even heard Sheriff Mallon sneak up behind. Mallon stood with a shovel in hand, toothpick in his mouth, taste of cinnamon on his tongue.

"You sure do have the tendency to scare the shit out of me, Sheriff. Be it sitting in your car down the road with your beady eyes, or feet above me with a shovel in your hand."

"Sorry about that."

"Listen to you, an apology." Calvin lifted himself out of the grave and sat on the edge, legs dangling.

The sheriff used the shovel to quickly carve a seat in one of the large mounds Calvin had built, then sat in it, set the shovel on the ground.

"If you've come to rub it in that Genie should've gone to the hospital, he knew what he was doing. This was the end he wanted, on his terms."

The sheriff offered a sympathetic smile, then extended an arm. In his hand was Genie's knife. "Thought you may want this. No sense in holding onto evidence that ain't needed."

Calvin took the knife, and his eyes grew wet.

"I think we need to clear something up, Calvin." The man huffed, then started again. "Deputy Wayne's sister, Kathryn . . . "

"Lady you were in love with."

Mallon looked surprised. "That's right . . . well, she died." He swallowed. His voice tremored slightly. "She was a real good woman. Her husband, not so much. Tim's dad was, well . . . Let's just say he was. Don't deserve further clarification." He cleared his throat and continued. "Her and I . . . it happened out of nowhere. Despite what you may think of me, I'm an honest man. Stealing another man's wife is a sin I thought I'd never face." He clammed up and stared ahead for a long moment.

"And you're telling me this why?"

"Because, other than an apology, I owe you an explanation. I don't hate you, Calvin. And I didn't hate your friend. He was an easy target for grief. Kathryn was a black woman. Most gorgeous woman you've ever seen. Heart of pure gold." A tight-lipped smile appeared as he reminisced. "But cancer took that beauty and that gold."

Calvin felt a stone drop in his gut at the ugly C-word he hoped he'd never hear again.

"For months she laid in bed, while her piece-of-shit husband did nothin' but hit the bar, looking for a piece of ass. I couldn't hold her. I couldn't be her rock. It's all I wanted. It's what she needed."

"I sympathize, Sheriff, but you're losing me. That's got nothing to do with me and Genie coming here."

Mallon nodded. "Your friend had cancer, didn't he?"

Calvin's brow furrowed. "And how would you know that?"

"I smelled it on him the day we met. And then him being black. Well . . . call it the perfect storm for some misdirected anger. I've spent the last two days trying to figure out why I came across as someone so shallow—"

"And so racist."

"Yes . . . and racist. And the only thing I can figure is I've put up a wall that guards my heart. It wasn't Genie, and it wasn't the color of him. It was the reminder that the woman I loved had suffered. She suffered more than she needed to because of that son of a bitch she married."

"And that's why you burned his house down . . . with him in it."

Mallon drove eyes right through Calvin, latched on. "And that's why I burned his house down . . . with him in it."

Calvin looked off, taking a moment to absorb it all. "The deputy knew, didn't he? That's what he had on you."

"That's right."

Calvin smiled, filled with a small amount of relief. "If Genie were down there right now," he nodded toward the grave, "he'd be rolling over, hearing you fess up like this."

"Two reasons why I'm trusting you, Calvin. One is the deep need to get it off my chest. The other, I know you fellas killed Tim's friend Andy."

Calvin swallowed hard, and his eyes displayed a guilt he couldn't hide.

"But more importantly, I know *why* you did it. And that's why you're not in the holding cell back at the station."

"Not much gets by you, does it, Sheriff?"

"It's my job."

"I'll keep it to myself, but I'll bet I can think of one egg you haven't found."

"If you're referring to Rosem's four-foot barren graves, I'm way ahead of you."

Calvin couldn't help but chuckle.

CHAPTER 56

THE TURNOUT FOR the funeral was few. A couple from the church Calvin and Genie had traded smiles with more than once, Sheriff Mallon, Pastor Rosem, and even Jimmy Rosem, who stood behind a distant tree and had somehow dressed for the occasion. Calvin was hoping Dottie and Denise would show but understood the young girl had her own grieving to do, having just lost her father, and of course Dottie's time now spent tucking the child under her wing.

Calvin thought of that poor girl and what she'd been through. He knew this wasn't the outcome she wanted. But at the very least, she was free from Tim now. There'd be scars, but no more fresh wounds.

He wanted to visit her, but now wasn't the time. Maybe a month from now, when things had settled and she was able to understand this new grief, begin to work through it. He'd bring her a new pad of paper and request the talent of her tracing, hang the ghost of Genie's stone on the wall near where he used to sit at the table, sipping on his coffee and reflecting on their blessings.

At the service, the pastor spoke of salvation and being free from sickness and suffering and how much better Genie has it now that he's gone. He talked about the Eugene MacDowell he felt he knew, which Calvin felt summed him up pretty well, though no mention of Genie's fragility when it came to loving others. Other than tornadoes, the man's biggest fear had been losing loved ones. It kept him up nights and was the reason for refusing to let go of Louise, pretending she still breathed somewhere near the bridge, knitting scarves and mittens for those in need.

When the tiny crowd dissolved, Calvin stood alone, shovel in one hand, Genie's ratty suitcase in the other. He shared with Genie everything Sheriff Mallon had told him and said he was thinking of sticking around, now that he realized the devil in their midst was nothing but a confused man who couldn't stop hurting, much like themselves.

Calvin opened the failing zipper on the suitcase and looked at the hundreds of letters contained inside, all addressed to Louise. He read none of them. Not once had he even been tempted to glance at the secret, mourning words. He just played along with the charade, knowing Genie knew the truth, that Louise really had died under that bridge and was in her own bed at Cheyenne Cemetery back in Chicago. But if writing letters to the dead kept his friend smiling, he would have written them too if Genie had asked.

He tipped the suitcase and let the words rain atop Genie's casket, pitter-pattering on its lid, then looked around the spot Genie had picked. The shady areas that kept the grass lush, the street light overhead that brought a comforting ambience in the wee hours, the neatly trimmed hedges nearby, the ones they'd complained grew like weeds. Genie had chosen well.

"Yeah . . . I think I'll stick around, brother. You once told me home is where you lay your head, wherever you have a friend, and wherever the sun warms you. I'd say that fits here pretty well." Calvin's voice wavered as his vision blurred. "See you soon, old man." And he turned away.

THE END?

Not if you want to dive into more of Crystal Lake Publishing's Tales from the Darkest Depths!

Check out our amazing website and online store
or download our latest catalog here.
https://geni.us/CLPCatalog

Looking for award-winning Dark Fiction?
Download our latest catalog.

Includes our anthologies, novels, novellas, collections,
poetry, non-fiction, and specialty projects.

WHERE STORIES COME ALIVE!

We always have great new projects and content on the website to dive into, as well as a newsletter, behind the scenes options, social media platforms, our own dark fiction shared-world series and our very own webstore. Our webstore even has categories specifically for KU books, non-fiction, anthologies, and of course more novels and novellas.

ABOUT THE AUTHORS

Full-time family man, artist, musician, and ferret owner with twenty books under his belt, Chad Lutzke dips his toe into all things dark: Crime, thrillers, noir, slice-of-life and horror, every one smothered in heartache with the occasional sliver of hope. Some of his books include: OF FOSTER HOMES & FLIES, STIRRING THE SHEETS, THE PALE WHITE, SKULLFACE BOY, THE SAME DEEP WATER AS YOU, THREE-SMILE MILE, and THE NEON OWL series. Lutzke's work has been praised by authors Jack Ketchum, Richard Chizmar, Joe R. Lansdale, Stephen Graham Jones, Tim Waggoner, and his own mother. He can be found lurking the internet at www.chadlutzke.com

John Boden was mostly raised in the mountains of Pennsylvania, in the small town of Orbisonia. He is a bakery manager by trade and finds a regular sleep schedule overrated. He currently resides with his beautiful wife and two sons, in a house sweetly haunted by the ghost of a beautician named, Darlene. He likes collecting lots of things and won't usually shut up about it. His writing is fairly well received and has been called unique of style. His work has been published in the form of stories in several anthologies and as novellas. He plays well with others as is evidenced by collaborative works with Mercedes M. Yardley, Bracken MacLeod, Kurt Newton, Brian Rosenberger, Chad Lutzke and Robert Ford. He's easy to track down either on Facebook or Twitter (JohnBoden1970)

Our Mission Statement:

Since its founding in August 2012, Crystal Lake Publishing has quickly become one of the world's leading publishers of Dark Fiction and Horror books in print, eBook, and audio formats.

While we strive to present only the highest quality fiction and entertainment, we also endeavour to support authors along their writing journey. We offer our time and experience in non-fiction projects, as well as author mentoring and services, at competitive prices.

With several Bram Stoker Award wins and many other wins and nominations (including the HWA's Specialty Press Award), Crystal Lake Publishing puts integrity, honor, and respect at the forefront of our publishing operations.

We strive for each book and outreach program we spearhead to not only entertain and touch or comment on issues that affect our readers, but also to strengthen and support the Dark Fiction field and its authors.

Not only do we find and publish authors we believe are destined for greatness, but we strive to work with men and women who endeavour to be decent human beings who care more for others than themselves, while still being hard working, driven, and passionate artists and storytellers.

Crystal Lake Publishing is and will always be a beacon of what passion and dedication, combined with overwhelming teamwork and respect, can accomplish. We endeavour to know each and every one of our readers, while building personal relationships with our authors, reviewers, bloggers, podcasters, bookstores, and libraries.

We will be as trustworthy, forthright, and transparent as any business can be, while also keeping most of the headaches away from our authors, since it's our job to solve the problems so they can stay in a creative mind. Which of course also means paying our authors.

We do not just publish books, we present to you worlds within your world, doors within your mind, from talented authors who sacrifice so much for a moment of your time.

There are some amazing small presses out there, and through collaboration and open forums we will continue to support other presses in the goal of helping authors and showing the world what quality small presses are capable of accomplishing. No one wins when a small press goes down, so we will always be there to support hardworking, legitimate presses and their authors. We don't see Crystal Lake as the best press out there, but we will always strive to be the best, strive to be the most interactive and grateful, and even blessed press around. No matter what happens over time, we will also take our mission very seriously while appreciating where we are and enjoying the journey.

What do we offer our authors that they can't do for themselves through self-publishing?

We are big supporters of self-publishing (especially hybrid publishing), if done with care, patience, and planning. However, not every author has the time or inclination to do market research, advertise, and set up book launch strategies. Although a lot of authors are successful in doing it all, strong small presses will always be there for the authors who just want to do what they do best: write.

What we offer is experience, industry knowledge, contacts and trust built up over years. And due to our strong brand and trusting fanbase, every Crystal Lake Publishing book comes with weight of respect. In time our fans begin to trust our judgment and will try a new author purely based on our support of said author.

With each launch we strive to fine-tune our approach, learn from our mistakes, and increase our reach. We continue to assure our authors that we're here for them and that we'll carry the weight of the launch and dealing with third parties while they focus on their strengths—be it writing, interviews, blogs, signings, etc.

We also offer several mentoring packages to authors that include knowledge and skills they can use in both traditional and self-publishing endeavours.

We look forward to launching many new careers.

This is what we believe in. What we stand for. This will be our legacy.

Welcome to Crystal Lake Publishing— Tales from the Darkest Depths.

Printed in the USA
CPSIA information can be obtained
at www.ICGtesting.com
JSHW010823200124
55549JS00005B/16

9 781957 133713